A Christmas miracle...

Deke had never, ever considered being part of a family—being a husband, a father.

All he remembered of his own family life was the tension between himself and his dad, his mother's inability to do more than wring her hands and the unhappiness that seemed to permeate the very air they breathed.

Of course, he knew that wasn't the way all families were—he'd seen families like his friend Erin's—but he'd always expected that misery was inevitable for any family he was part of.

Yet now, tonight, for the first time, Deke began to wonder if he could make a go of it.

He wondered if he could make a go of it with Erin. With her three kids. With his new son.

And Deke noticed with wonderment that it was beginning to look a lot like Christmas....

Chapter 1

"Da," the little boy in the car seat said. He bounced himself against the restraining belt that anchored him, clapped his hands together and grinned. "Da," he said again, testing the word, frowning as if it didn't sound quite right. "Daaaaa…" he tried again. "Da-da…" Then at last, "Da…d."

And he beamed his triumph at the man driving the pickup—his father.

Me, Deke Malone thought, his gaze flicking to the boy in the rearview mirror, his fingers strangling the steering wheel.

Even after three months' time, the notion still occasionally had the effect of poleaxing him.

He was a *father.* Two and a half years ago he had contributed unknowingly to the conception of a child. *This* child.

This beautiful, wonderful, nearly twenty-month-old boy whose existence he had never imagined—especially not that August afternoon three months ago when a stranger had appeared on his doorstep.

She had looked proper and official in her dark skirt and pale-blue blouse, not at all like the usual photographer's groupies or wanna-bes who occasionally turned up to knock on Deke's door now that his work was well-known.

She was, she'd said, Mrs. Trammell from some department of social services or child welfare or something he'd never heard of before. He'd said she must have the wrong house.

But she had consulted the sheaf of papers in her hand, then looked up and asked if he was Mr. Malone? "Mr. Daniel Kevin Malone?"

"That's right," Deke said, still mystified.

And she had smiled at him. "I've brought your son."

For a moment the word had meant nothing to him. Son? It wasn't even a part of his active vocabulary. Deke wasn't a family man. Had no intention of ever becoming one. But as the word echoed in his head, it connected with the preceding one: *your*…and the meaning began to register.

Deke took a quick step back, holding up his palms in denial. "*Son? My* son? Ho, no! No, ma'am. No way. You've got the wrong guy. I don't have a son."

But Mrs. Trammell assured him that he had.

Deke hadn't believed her.

"Who's the mother?" he'd demanded, certain it was a mistake. Not that it was impossible, just extremely unlikely. He'd slept with women in his lifetime, but there hadn't been many and he'd always been careful. Very careful. Deke wasn't a fool and he didn't sleep around. The women he slept with were no more interested in having a family than he was.

Mrs. Trammell consulted her paperwork again. "Her name was Violet Ashton."

"Violet?"

That was almost more stunning.

Violet Ashton had had his child? The Violet who'd climbed Everest? Who'd ridden camels in Marrakesh? Who'd spent a season at the South Pole?

For three years running Violet Ashton had been named Adventure Photographer of the Year by one of the biggest trade publications in the outdoor recreation field. The same Violet had once confided to him that her primary goal in life was to go as many places and do—and shoot—as many things as she possibly could. Not exactly Mom of the Year material.

In fact, in the dozen or so times Violet had breezed through his life in the past ten years, Deke had never heard her express any interest in having a child.

He'd always liked Violet. And one of the things he'd liked best about her—besides the fact that she approached sex with the same enthusiasm with which she approached kayaking down the Mackenzie or climbing Kilimanjaro—was that she'd never been any more interested in home and family than he had.

"What are you talking about?" he'd demanded of the woman standing on his doorstep. "Where the hell is Violet?"

Mrs. Trammell must have majored in patience. She took a slow, calm breath and answered his first question. She was, she told him, talking about a seventeen-month-old boy named Isaac Daniel Ashton.

His son. And Violet's.

"You're listed as his father on his birth certificate," she told him, shuffling through more papers and finally pulling out an official-looking document. She handed it to him.

He stared at it.

In the meantime Mrs. Trammell went on to answer his second question. Another slow calm breath, followed by a sad smile this time. She was very sorry to have to tell him that Violet was dead.

Deke's gaze jerked up to meet hers. *"Dead?"*

"She drowned two weeks ago in Chile. She'd gone there on assignment for some magazine. We just got Zack back."

"Who's Zack?"

"Isaac," Mrs. Trammell had explained patiently. "Your son. Isaac Daniel. She called him Zack."

Deke hadn't taken it all in.

But eventually, of course, he had—because Mrs. Trammell hadn't gone away. She'd come in and sat down and laid all of her papers out on the table for him. The baby's birth certificate. Violet's death certificate. A sworn affidavit from a friend of hers declaring that, indeed, Violet had told her that Daniel "Deke" Malone was the father of her child.

He had the birth certificate memorized now. Isaac Daniel Ashton had been born in San Antonio, Texas, on April 24 of last year at 1:13 p.m. He'd weighed 8 lbs. 5 oz. and had been 21 inches long. His mother was Violet Mary Ashton. His father was…Daniel Kevin Malone.

"Dad!" Zack affirmed happily now, tossing a block at his father's ear. "Dad! Dad! Dad!"

Deke glanced back once more to see Zack grin at

him, then arch his back, as if he could push his way out of the car seat.

They'd have to stop soon. They'd been driving all day, and Zack didn't do long stretches gladly. Deke had found that out yesterday, two hours after they'd left Santa Fe.

Two hours in a car seat was pretty much the little boy's limit. Then he needed to get out and run around. He needed to eat, to roll on the ground, to grab his father's hands and scale his legs, then clamber up and ride on Deke's shoulders as they explored the rest stop.

It didn't matter to Deke. He was in no hurry.

They were in Wyoming now, near the Montana border. They'd passed the turnoff to the town near his sister Dori and brother-in-law Riley's ranch a couple of hours back. He hadn't stopped because Dori and Riley and their kids were on their way to Livingston, too.

Everybody was coming to the first—and undoubtedly last—Malone family Thanksgiving dinner. The very thought made Deke's stomach clench.

"Dad! Cookie, Da!" Zack demanded.

"You want to stop and eat lunch?" Deke asked. To Zack almost everything edible was a cookie. "Guess we can do that."

It would put off the inevitable a while longer.

They stopped at the next town. Deke bought Zack a carton of milk and made them each a cheese sandwich. He changed Zack's diaper and then took him to a small local park where he pushed him on the swing for ten minutes before they got back in the truck again and headed north. And his sense of foreboding returned.

Of course he hadn't had to come. No one was holding a gun to his head. His parents weren't even expecting him. Why should they be? He hadn't been home in fifteen years.

But Milly, his youngest sister, the family peacemaker, had called him last month and invited him.

"Dori and Riley are coming," she'd said, "and the kids. You could meet Carrie." Their daughter, she meant. "And C.J." Her own son whom he hadn't ever seen either. C.J. was a couple months younger than Zack.

"Well, I—"

"And, for that matter, you could meet Cash and Riley," Milly went on relentlessly. His two brothers-in-law.

Deke had missed both his sisters' weddings, claiming to have photo assignments that prevented him from making it. In fact, he could have, but he chose not to.

He hadn't wanted to make things even more tense than weddings already were by turning up on a festive occasion and creating family tension instead. He'd figured maybe Dori and Milly would bring their husbands and come see him, but so far they hadn't.

"And we," Milly went on determinedly, "could finally meet Zack. We want to meet Zack, Deke."

Milly knew about Zack. Dori knew about Zack. His mother knew about Zack. Probably most of Montana—even his father—knew about Zack by now.

But Deke hadn't told anyone about Zack right away. He'd needed to get used to the idea of having a son himself first.

He hadn't had the faintest idea how to be a father. He'd never changed a diaper or spooned oatmeal into a waiting mouth. He'd never paced the floor with a crying child or felt parental panic at a spiking fever or ill at the sight of blood.

Not then. But he'd learned. Fast.

He was on a first-name basis with a pediatrician now. He had been to the hospital emergency room with a screaming child, been patted on the head and reassured by a trio of long-suffering nurses. He'd felt like an idiot—but had been so vastly relieved when they'd told him teething was all that had been making Zack scream that he hadn't cared about appearing idiotic at all.

He loved being a father. He loved the little boy who wrapped his neck in a tight hug, who laughed at his animal noises, who wept tears on his shirtfront, who peed on his bare feet.

And he'd found himself wondering at odd moments if his own father had ever felt any of those things.

Two of a kind—stubborn hard-nosed men—John and Deke Malone had fought many a battle with each other while Deke was growing up. If Deke had been the apple of his father's eye when he was young, all that had begun to change when he'd got a mind—and goals—of his own.

Deke had loved the outdoors, the wide-open spaces, horses and cattle, and the simple little camera his mother's father had given him. It had given him a new way of seeing the world—and he'd seen that he didn't want to spend it working in the family grocery store.

His father had disagreed.

The disagreements had escalated through Deke's high school years. They'd worsened during his time at Montana State. The last one had taken place fifteen years ago, not long after Deke graduated. He'd told his father he was thinking about going to Paris to pursue his study of photography. He could remember it now. It was as if he'd said he was going to be an astronaut or president of the United States.

John had stared at him over the side of beef he was carving, then he'd shaken his head and told Deke to stop talking nonsense and sort the brussels sprouts.

It had been the last straw.

He'd ripped off his butcher's apron and stalked out.

He'd never been back. He'd left home that night, had taken jobs where he could find them, had taken photos when he could. He and his father hadn't spoken since that day. And Deke had rarely thought of him until he'd held Zack in his arms.

When he did, he couldn't imagine that his father had ever felt for him anything close to the intense love he felt for Zack. Or maybe he just hadn't wanted to imagine.

Over the past three months, he'd begun to wonder.

What had it been like for his father? John Malone had been barely twenty-one when Deke was born. He'd already been working in the store alongside his own father. When he'd held his son in his arms, what had he hoped for? Deke didn't know. Couldn't even guess.

Memories came back. Not just those of the later fights and arguments, but earlier ones, happier ones. Ones he had forgotten, that pricked at him and made him wonder. What was the old man like now?

Would they understand each other any better than they ever had? Could they ever make peace? Did he want to?

Surprising himself, Deke took Milly's invitation.

"But don't tell the folks we're coming," he'd warned.

"In case you chicken out?"

"I'm not going to chicken out," Deke had replied, stung, even though God knew he'd been tempted often enough to do just that in the month since he'd agreed. He told himself it was a very bad idea and still felt this compulsion to go. Probably it was both—a bad idea *and* a compulsion.

He glanced in the rearview mirror now. Zack's eyes were closed. He was asleep, his worn stuffed dog, Beero, in his arms.

So they didn't have to stop again. They'd surely make Livingston by nightfall now, and he'd come face-to-face with his father for the first time in fifteen years—the prodigal son come home.

But one thing he was damned sure of—as far as John Malone was concerned, there would be no fatted calf and no celebration.

The house looked just the same.

It was a wood frame story-and-a-half bungalow with dormers, built in the first quarter of the last century. It was painted white—there was no other color as far as John Malone was concerned—and had a deep front porch that spanned its entire width.

"We're here, buddy," Deke said, lifting Zack out of his car seat. The little boy looked curiously at all the white stuff on the ground. They'd had only a flurry or two in Santa Fe so far this year. Already there was half a foot of snow in Livingston on the ground.

Deke scooped some snow up and held it so Zack could touch it. The little boy's eyes widened at the cold on his fingers. He grinned, then poked his fingers in it again. "Cream?" he said hopefully.

Deke shook his head. "Not ice cream. Snow. We'll

build a snowman." Zack looked puzzled. "I'll show you," Deke promised. It was one of the wonderful bits of being a father—enjoying everything anew, treasuring the wonder on his son's face. He would have liked to set the boy down right then and build the snowman for him.

But that would be postponing the inevitable. Postponing his father.

He mounted the steps.

"Da!" Zack wriggled fretfully in his arms, and he realized his grip on the boy had tightened. Deliberately he eased his hold and balanced Zack on his hip. Then, taking one more deep breath, Deke knocked on the door.

He waited, shifted from one foot to the other, felt like a fool for knocking on the door of the house he'd grown up in, yet knew he couldn't just walk in.

The porch light came on. Beyond the glass of the storm door, the front door opened slowly and his mother's astonished eyes widened as she stared at him.

Deke grinned faintly, hopefully. "Hey, Ma."

For just a second she didn't move. Then she made a sound somewhere between a soft shriek and a moan and she shoved the door open.

"Oh, my! Oh, my God, Deke!" She started to hug him, stepped back and looked at the little boy in his arms. Her eyes filled with tears. "This is…Zack?"

"This is Zack," Deke agreed. "This is your grandma," he told his son.

Zack looked at her, wide-eyed, as Carol Malone gathered both of them close in a hard fierce hug. And Deke knew that, regardless of how his father felt about his arrival, he was right to have come. He'd seen his mother only a handful of times since he'd left—when she and Milly or she and Dori and Jake had come to visit him in Santa Fe. Then she'd put on her best face and acted as if it was all a wonderful holiday. Now he could see in her unguarded expression as she looked at him how much pain there had been.

She dabbed at her eyes and shook her head. "You just don't know…" she began, then stopped and went up on tiptoe to kiss Deke's cheek while she stroked Zack's soft hair. "I never dared hope… You're both so stubborn."

His father, she meant. And him.

"*We're* not," Deke said flatly, his words encompassing himself and his son.

His mother didn't reply, just drew the two of them into the house. "He's in the den watching basketball. He'll be glad to see you."

Deke raised a doubtful brow.

"He will," she insisted, "though he might not admit it."

"Surprise, surprise," Deke said under his breath.

"He doesn't always show his feelings."

On the contrary, Deke thought. John Malone had often shown his feelings far too well. "You don't have to explain him, Mom. I remember what he's like."

But he wasn't prepared for the man he saw.

It might only have been fifteen years since he'd seen his father, but he looked as if it had been fifty. Deke had often referred to his father as "the old man" without really meaning the adjective or thinking of his father as old.

But the man in the recliner was definitely that.

He wouldn't be sixty for two more years, but his hair was snow-white. He'd been broad-shouldered and sturdy in the old days. Now he looked gaunt, almost frail and far older than his years.

Deke knew his father had suffered a serious heart attack six years ago. But he'd bounced back and within weeks had insisted on going back to work full-time at the store, much to his daughters' dismay. They'd told Deke repeatedly that it had aged him. Deke had thought they were exaggerating.

Apparently not, he thought, stopping in the doorway to the den.

"John," Deke's mother said brightly, "look who's here."

His father turned his head, starting to smile. Then he saw who it was and his expression became flat, shuttered and remote—as if a door had been firmly shut. He didn't speak.

"It's Deke," his mother said a little desperately, "and Zack."

As if the old man didn't know, Deke thought. He still hadn't moved.

At the sound of his name, though, the little boy grinned and bounced in his arms. Thank God someone was impervious to the tension vibrating in the room.

"Da!" Zack said cheerfully, and reached up to wrap his small arms around Deke's neck. "Dad!"

John Malone's gaze flickered again. A muscle ticked in his jaw. He looked from Zack to Deke.

"Dad," Deke said after a moment, measuring his tone, aiming for polite, but not eager or desperate. His voice sounded rusty and his throat felt tight, but he was damned if he'd clear it. He simply stared straight ahead, meeting his father's gaze and wondering if the old man would say what he'd said fifteen years ago. *Get out.*

Deke could hear his mother's nervous breathing. He

seriously debated turning on his heel and heading back out the door.

But then, at last, his father dipped his head slightly. "Deke."

It was the barest of acknowledgments. Deke stopped holding his breath.

But before he could speak, his father cleared his voice and went on gruffly. "Don't go expectin' your mother to take care of that boy because you haven't got a wife."

Deke's jaw dropped. Then he clamped his teeth together so it wouldn't, but mostly so he wouldn't voice any of half a dozen furious retorts. How infuriatingly typical of his father to make that assumption. *Don't take advantage.* As if that was the reason he'd come back.

"He isn't asking me to take care of Zack," Carol said, her fingers strangling each other. "They came for a visit. For Thanksgiving, didn't you, Deke?" She turned desperate eyes on him.

Deke had to work to get his jaw to move. When he finally did, he said stonily, "We came for a visit." His voice didn't sound rusty to his own ears now. Or pleasant. It sounded hard—like his old man's heart.

Why the hell had he bothered?

"We're so glad you're here," his mother babbled on. "Dori and Riley and the kids got here this afternoon. They're out at Milly's now. But you can have your old room and—"

"No," Deke cut in swiftly, his voice harsh, then gentling. "Thanks, Mom, but no. Milly said we could stay there. We'll stay with Milly and Cash."

If he'd thought he would get an argument, he was wrong. His mother actually looked relieved.

That made two of them, Deke thought.

Carol smiled. "Well, that's lovely, dear. You'll be more comfortable there. There will be more room, I mean," she corrected herself hastily. "And Zack will have C.J. to play with. It would have been crowded here, but we would have managed, wouldn't we, John?"

But John Malone wasn't paying any attention to them. He had turned back to the basketball game.

Deke was halfway to Joneses' ranch before he realized what he was doing.

It was, of course, where he'd been headed, anyway— to spend the night with Milly and Cash in the small tenant house they occupied on the Jones family spread. But he hadn't been thinking about Milly and Cash at all when he'd kissed his mother goodbye and bundled Zack in the truck and headed out again.

He'd been thinking about his father, about the less-than-enthusiastic reception the old man had given them, and how he would never understand John Malone if he lived to be a hundred.

It wasn't as if Deke was a failure, for God's sake, as if he'd turned his back on the family only to bring them shame.

He might not be Ansel Adams, but he had a reasonable reputation in the photographic world. His work was admired, occasionally even esteemed. He taught masters classes in half a dozen photography schools around the country and was on the staff of a prestigious art institute in Santa Fe. He'd fulfilled his dream of buying a ranch. It wasn't a big one, but he ran cattle on a small spread not far outside Santa Fe.

Wasn't that better than sorting brussels sprouts for

the rest of his life? Wasn't that better than wasting his talents?

Apparently not. The only thing John Malone seemed to value was blind obedience to his will.

Deke slammed his fist against the steering wheel and took a bend in the road a little too quickly—the same bend he always used to take too quickly when he'd been on his way to see Erin.

And that was when he realized what he was doing.

He'd had a battle with his father. He was angry and out of sorts. He needed someone to talk to, someone who would settle him down, listen to him mutter, steer him straight.

And that was Erin Jones.

He lifted his foot off the accelerator, took a deep breath and smiled just a little as he remembered Erin now. From the day he'd met her in his last year of high school, Erin had been his confidante, his soul mate, his friend.

He'd always thought of her as the "kid sister" who was closer to him than either of his real sisters had been—even closer than Milly, who had followed him around since she'd been born. Because for all that Milly had hero-worshiped him and he'd basked in it willingly, he'd never been able to let down his guard with Milly. You didn't with somebody who thought you were a hero.

Erin didn't think that. She'd always been his biggest supporter—but she knew he was no hero. He'd been little more than a boy trying to be a man when he'd met her. Erin had helped him find the courage to do it.

He remembered the day he'd met her as if it were yesterday. She and her dad had come into the grocery store one afternoon just in time to catch him on the receiving end of one of John Malone's "stop your daydreaming and do your work" lectures, which had left Deke both embarrassed and furious.

He'd wanted to sink through the floor when he recognized Will Jones, one of the biggest ranchers in the county, standing there with his pretty teenage daughter, both of them almost as embarrassed as he'd been at being forced to witness every word of the dressing-down his dad had given him.

But before he could bolt into the back room, the girl had said, "Aren't you Deke Malone?"

His father, still glowering, had muttered, "As if there could be another one," in a gruff disgusted tone.

But the girl just said eagerly, "I saw your photos at Dusty's place. They're fantastic."

Deke had been amazed. No one else had noticed the dozen photos of an elk hunt he'd hung at Dusty's Art and Bait Shop the week before. His father had snorted something about "showing off" when Deke had told him about it. "Gettin' too big for your britches," he'd said.

And it seemed he might be right because no one had seemed to notice. Until now. Getting someone else's approval stunned him.

And it was that approval, Deke was sure, that had given him the courage to follow Will Jones out to his truck to try to talk the older man into hiring him as a cowboy for the summer. It had been a brash, foolish thing to do. He could ride a horse. He could build a loop. But his skills with cattle were nonexistent. He had no experience—except selling groceries.

But he'd dreamed of cowboying almost as much as he'd dreamed of taking pictures. And another summer spent inside the stifling grocery store under his father's disapproving eye was more than he could stand. He'd known he couldn't make enough money taking photos to support himself, but he had to get out of the store, had to be outside, had to escape.

"I'll work so hard you won't need to hire anybody else," he'd sworn fervently.

Will hadn't looked thrilled. He'd scratched his head and shrugged his shoulders. He hadn't said yes. He'd said, "I'll think about it."

Deke had gone back inside, embarrassed by his eagerness and his father's quick dismissal of the idea.

"What do you know about cowboying?" he'd challenged when Deke had come back inside.

"Not much," Deke had admitted.

"Foolishness," his father had said. "You've got responsibilities right here."

Not ones he'd wanted, though. But he'd figured he'd be stuck with them, so he'd been stunned that night when Will Jones had called and offered to take him on.

"Not sure you'll be the only hand I'll have to hire," Will had said with a smile in his voice, "But I like a fella who's eager, and I reckon you'll learn something."

"Yes, sir!" Deke had said earnestly, still amazed at his good fortune.

It wasn't until the end of the summer that he'd realized that Erin had been the one to talk her father into it. She had always been his advocate, his supporter, his friend. They had been on the same wavelength from the moment they'd met. Erin had been a photographer, too, she'd told him. But she'd never been brave enough to ask Dusty to display her pictures.

"Or desperate enough," Deke had said.

Erin had laughed. "Maybe that's it. Or maybe," she'd said humbly, "I'm just not as good as you."

But she was. Deke had learned that quick enough.

She was every bit as good with a camera as he was. While he focused on landscapes, Erin concentrated on people. They complemented each other, they challenged each other. They talked and argued and teased and supported each other.

It was a wonderful summer—the best of his life. Erin was talented and smart and compassionate. She worked long, hard hours all summer long. And after that, even though in the fall he'd gone to college and still had to work in the store and she'd gone back to high school and they hadn't seen each other every day, whenever he felt hemmed in, he went to talk to Erin.

She settled him, calmed him, gave him some perspective. She always listened. She made sense of things for him. He talked to her about everything—his hopes, his troubles, his old man, his dreams. He even talked to her about the girls he dated because she was so sane, so sensible, so unlike all of them!

"You have more girlfriends than my dad has cattle," she'd told him once.

He'd grinned. "Safety in numbers."

She'd socked him lightly on the arm. "You're awful."

He'd shaken his head. "I'm not! I'm trying to find one who'll understand me."

She'd rolled her eyes. "Good luck."

Sometimes, when Deke looked back on it, he thought that the only one who had was Erin.

Apparently, twenty years later, he must still think so because instinctively he'd headed toward the ranch.

For all the good it would do him.

Erin was gone. Had been for years. It was Erin who had actually gone to Paris to study photography at the end of her senior year of college. It was Erin who had suggested he come, too. He'd been stamping cereal boxes at the time, still trying to balance his "responsibilities" with his "dreams."

"Yeah, sure," he'd said, annoyed that she made it sound so easy. "Like I can afford to just pack up and move to Paris."

"You could," she'd said, "if you—" But then she'd stopped. Her expression grew shuttered. The easy openness he was so used to was suddenly no longer there.

"If I what?" he'd pressed her.

"Nothing. Never mind." And she'd pasted on the first artificial smile he'd ever seen on her face. "Whatever."

It had been the last thing she'd said to him.

She hadn't come to say goodbye. When he'd got some time off on the weekend and had gone up to see her, her mother said she'd already left. She'd been as surprised as Deke that Erin hadn't come to say goodbye to him.

"Ah, well," Gaye Jones had said with a gentle smile, "she probably thought it was best this way. She might have cried, you know. Erin gets a little sentimental."

"Yeah," Deke said, feeling out of sorts. But probably it had been better. For her.

And maybe for him. He'd had the blowup with his father soon after, and Erin hadn't been there to blunt his fury. With no one there to calm him down or make him see reason, he did exactly what she'd done—for entirely different reasons—he'd left town.

And in the end, it was the best thing that could have happened to him.

Erin, too, Milly had told him later. She'd got married to a French journalist. She'd stayed in Paris, had had kids there. Over the years he'd seen a little of her work. She still shot people, capturing their emotions, their reactions, their hopes and joys and fears.

Every once in a while, when he saw one of her photos that he particularly liked, Deke had been tempted to drop her a note and say so. He never had. It seemed presumptuous. She might not even remember him.

Two years ago her husband had died—victim of a fire fight in the Middle East while he was covering a story. Milly had told him that, too. Deke had heard about the fighting, but he hadn't realized it was Erin's husband who'd been killed.

When he found out, he'd considered writing her a letter of condolence. He hadn't done that either. Too many years had passed.

You can't go home again. Wasn't that what they said?

But apparently some part of Deke's brain had thought he could, had at least been determined to try. Tonight, in the aftermath of his encounter with his father, he had instinctively headed straight for Joneses' ranch, ready to pour out his frustration to Erin—to Erin who wasn't even there.

Chapter 2

The welcome Deke got from his sisters went a long way toward improving his mood.

They shrieked and screamed and threw their arms around him and Zack the minute he walked in the door. Laughing, yet feeling oddly emotional himself, Deke hugged them back, delighted that they looked happy and that married life and motherhood seemed to be agreeing with both of them.

"I'll have to go away more often," he said with a grin. "You were never this glad to see me when we were growing up."

"One hopes you have grown up," Dori said darkly. "No more bugs in our beds."

"No more cold cream on the toilet seat," Milly added.

"Shh! Don't give Jake ideas," Dori cautioned her

sister, with a wary look in the direction of her ten-year-old son.

Jake's eyes were shining. "Did you really?" he asked his uncle Deke.

Deke grinned. "Only a few times. Holy cow, you've gotten big!" Jake was taller than his elbow now. The boy hadn't reached Deke's belt the last time he and Dori had come to visit him in New Mexico. "Good grief. How old are you? Eighteen?"

"He wishes," Dori said, and ruffled her son's dark hair.

"Ten," Jake said, beaming up at his uncle. "I'm ten."

That was hard enough to believe. "I hear you've got a baby sister now," Deke said.

"Yep. Carrie. And I got a dad. Riley's my official dad, not just an uncle anymore," Jake said, grabbing his former uncle, now adoptive father, by the hand and dragging him forward to meet Deke. It was hard to tell which one he was more proud of—his brand-new little sister or the lean, dark-haired man who was now his dad.

"Glad to meet you at last," Deke said, shaking Riley Stratton's hand.

Riley nodded. "Likewise. Jake talks a lot about you. Cold cream, huh?" He grinned and tossed his wife a speculative glance. "Never thought of that."

"And you won't think of it again," Dori said sweetly, "or you'll be sorry."

The two of them looked at each other and a whole host of unspoken messages arced between them. Twitching lips turned to grins, then to outright laughter.

Riley looped an arm over Dori's shoulders and gave her a hug. "Would I do a thing like that?"

"No," she said promptly, "or I would be forced to tell everyone about your experience at the swimming hole."

"What experience?" Jake demanded.

"Swimming hole?" Milly said. "You never told me about any swimming hole." She looked at her sister avidly.

Riley was turning a definite shade of red. Deke raised his eyebrows at his sister.

But Dori grinned in satisfaction "No. Sorry. I think the toilet seat will be safe at our house."

"Mom!" Jake protested.

But Dori just shook her head. Before Jake could pester her further, the door opened and a cowboy came in, his arms full of loaves of bread and a little boy about the same size as Zack. The two little boys took one look at each other and beamed.

"Uh-oh," Milly said. "Double trouble." She turned to Deke. "This is C.J.—and Cash."

Cash was Milly's husband, a former rough stock rider who now worked for Taggart Jones and Noah Tanner teaching rodeo wanna-bes how to ride. And when he wasn't doing that he was taking classes at MSU, working in the biology lab and studying to become a vet.

"Hey, there," he said to Deke now, shaking his hand, grinning and giving Zack a wink at the same time. "Glad to meet you at last How ya doin', buddy?" he said to Zack. "Want to play with your cousin?"

Zack understood all about the word *play*. His wariness at his aunts' eager hugging vanished and he grinned, too, and wriggled to get down out of Deke's arms. "Play," he announced.

C.J. apparently understood the term, as well. "Truck,"

he said as his father set him down and the two ran off in the direction of a low set of shelves loaded with toy trucks, tractors and farm equipment.

"Get your stuff," Milly commanded Deke. "I made soup. It's on the back of the stove keeping warm. Cash and C.J. just went to Joneses' to bring back some of Felicity's pumpkin bread. She said she'd made too much for their Thanksgiving dinner tomorrow and wanted us to share."

Felicity, Deke knew, was Taggart's wife. Another new addition to the community whom he'd never met. There were so many new faces—Riley, Cash, Carrie, and C.J. just for starters—that he felt as if he'd been away forever. And yet being in the same room with his sisters again, laughing and teasing and recalling boyhood pranks, made him feel oddly as if no time had passed at all.

He went out to the truck to get his and Zack's gear, smiling, feeling good. The memory of his father's less-than-enthusiastic welcome faded.

Tomorrow it would be different. Tomorrow they would talk. He would show his father the books he'd done, photos he'd taken. He'd make the old man proud, make him see that he'd done better than he would have if he'd stayed at the store, that he'd done the right thing.

He got his and Zack's duffel bags out of the truck, balanced Beero on top of them and carried them back to the house.

From the sofa, Dori looked up and smiled at him. "You stayed away too long."

"Yes, you did," Milly chimed in. "You can't do that again. I'll expect you back in May."

Deke dumped the duffels beside the couch. "What's May?"

Milly beamed. "C.J.'s sibling is going to be born."

"What? Another one?" Dori obviously hadn't known this, either. "Are you sure?"

Milly rolled her eyes. "Of course I'm sure. I've done the test and seen the doc. Besides," she added, "I'm exhausted all the time and I'm puking my guts up every morning."

"Sit down," Dori commanded. She was nursing Carrie, but she moved over to make room for her sister. "You, too," she said to Deke. "Grab a cup of coffee or a bowl of soup and come talk to us."

Riley and Cash were deep in discussion about doctoring cattle. Jake was building a tower so the little boys could knock it down. Zack was enthralled and making brmmm-brmmm noises with the tractor as he anticipated it.

So Deke got a cup of coffee and joined his sisters, looking at the baby at Dori's breast, thinking how small she was—only three weeks old—and trying to imagine Zack that small. Had Violet nursed Zack? he wondered. There were so many things he didn't know.

Dori stuck her foot out and kicked his shin lightly. "So, big brother, who never wanted to be a father, how's it going?"

"Good."

She cocked her head. "Just good?"

Deke shook his head, unable to hide his smile. "No, not just good. Better."

He told them about Zack—about the panicky first days of fatherhood, about his dash to the emergency room, about Zack's new words and fascination with horses and his love of crayons.

"He likes to eat them, you mean?" Dori said. "When Dad gave Jake crayons, he ate them."

Deke shook his head. "No, he draws with them."

Both his sisters stared at him. "He's, what, eighteen months old?" Milly said doubtfully.

"Twenty," Deke said. "Almost twenty-one. I know. He's precocious. He just loves to draw."

"Draw what?"

Deke shrugged. "Who knows. It's abstract."

"Impressionist?" Dori grinned.

"Hard to say. He just spends a lot of time at it. Picking up one, then the other, scribbling on the page. But he doesn't get bored. I've got a whole portfolio of 'em," he admitted.

They looked at him, then at each other.

"The doting father," Milly said, grinning. "Who'd a thunk it?"

"Fatherhood seems to agree," Dori said with a grin.

Deke nodded. "A lot more than I figured it would."

"Speaking of which—" Milly prodded him with her toe "—did you stop and see ours?"

"Briefly." He didn't want to get into that now. Didn't even want to think about it.

"Oh, dear." Dori read between the lines.

"Don't worry. He'll come around." Milly curled her feet under her in the armchair. "He'll love Zack. He's wonderful with C.J."

"He was wonderful with Jake," Dori added, "until the business about Jake inheriting half the ranch came up."

Deke remembered hearing about how wonderful the

old man had been with his first grandchild. The sun had risen and set on Jake for years, according to an astonished Dori.

It wasn't until Riley had turned up to tell them that Jake had inherited half the Stratton family ranch after his father's death, that John Malone had started on the "duty and responsibility and the family store" stuff he used to shove down Deke's throat. He'd wanted Dori to sell Jake's inheritance and put it into the store. It would, after all, he'd told Dori, be Jake's some day.

Jake's reaction to the news had been no more enthusiastic than his uncle's had. He didn't want the store, he'd told his mother. He wanted the ranch.

John Malone had been appalled.

Dori had been willing to swallow her dreams in order to give Jake a future. But even when her father insisted, she hadn't been willing to destroy Jake's dreams and sell the ranch.

Instead she'd quit the store and Dori and Jake had moved in with Riley at the ranch. Deke didn't know the whole story about Dori and Riley on the ranch. But presumably something had happened at a swimming hole and a few months later they'd got married.

They'd been happily married now for over two years. They had a brand-new baby daughter, a thriving son. And apparently they'd made their peace with John Malone.

So it could be done.

"It's just so great you've come," Milly said now. "We'll have Thanksgiving dinner tomorrow like a real family—all of us together at last—the way it's supposed to be. Everything will be perfect. You'll see."

Deke devoutly hoped so.

* * *

Milly had brought the cranberry sauce, and the yams and the pumpkin pies.

"Good cranberry sauce," their father said, beaming down the table at his daughter. "Just like Grandma used to make."

Dori had brought banana and cranberry quick breads and the homemade apple butter she'd put up this fall.

"Always liked apple butter," their father said, adding a dollop to one of the hot rolls their mother had baked.

Deke had brought three bottles of a private label wine from a friend's vineyard.

John Malone stared at glasses his wife was filling. "Since when," he asked, "do we have wine at Thanksgiving?"

"Deke brought it from New Mexico," Carol said quickly. "It's from a local vineyard, isn't it, dear?" she asked him.

Deke mustered a smile. "That's right."

He didn't remember them ever having apple butter either. But he didn't say so. Instead he turned to Riley. "Pass the mashed potatoes, will you?"

Riley passed them. "Great potatoes." He gave Carol a bright smile. "It isn't Thanksgiving without mashed potatoes and gravy."

"Deke always mashes the potatoes," Carol said, as if he'd been here to do it every year. Certainly he'd done it this year. His mother had handed him the mixer that evening just as if he'd never been away. And Deke had taken it gladly, accepting it in the spirit it was offered—as a welcome back into the fold.

"Had 'em when he wasn't here," John Malone said flatly.

Tension simmered around the table. You could hear C.J. blow bubbles in his milk. Carefully, almost studiously, Deke spooned a small mound of mashed potatoes onto Zack's plate. He didn't look his father's way.

He'd tried smiling when they'd come in that afternoon. He'd said, "Hey, Dad, how are you?" and had deliberately taken Zack over to him. "This is your grandpa. Say hi to your grandpa."

Zack, bless his heart, had said, "Hi," and given his grandpa a big smile.

To give the old man credit, he'd smiled in return. He'd ruffled the boy's hair and chucked him under the chin. He'd never met Deke's eyes, and had almost at once made some excuse about needing to get something in the basement and had slipped down the stairs and away.

He hadn't reappeared until dinner was served. Then he'd taken his place at the head of the table, looked at them all—save Deke—with satisfaction and had proceeded to make his pronouncements on the meal. Milly and Dori tried to paper over the awkwardness of his remarks. Their mother smiled with all her might and tried to pretend everything was lovely.

And Deke felt steam coming out his ears.

"More turkey, anyone?" Carol asked brightly.

"I'll have some," Cash said quickly. He took the platter. "Deke?"

"Sure." Though it tasted like rubber to him. He turned to his brother-in-law. "So tell me, how's it going at the bull-and bronc-riding school?"

"Goin' good. Real good." It didn't seem to bother him that he was limping from getting kicked by a bull yesterday. "Got a bunch of eager kids out there right now. Gotta be eager," he reflected wryly, "to spend your entire Thanksgiving riding broncs or bulls."

"It's called dedication," Riley said with a grin. "We all had it once."

"We still do," Cash said, "we're just focusing on different stuff." He grimaced. "Two weeks and I've got finals coming up."

They talked about his classes and then about the work he was doing for Taggart and Noah. "It's a nice break," he said. "You ought to come visit while you're here. You know Taggart, don't you?"

"Oh, yeah. Worked for Will one summer."

"Come tonight," Milly invited.

"Yeah," Cash agreed. "They're having the annual Thanksgiving bash up at Taggart's. All the cowboys from the school, a bunch of locals. You probably knew some of them. Maybe you can get a few to turn up at your opening."

"What opening?" Deke's mother asked him.

"Deke's got a show opening at Dustin's tomorrow night," Milly said, looking at her mother, surprised. "Didn't he tell you?"

Carol shook her head and looked at Deke for an explanation.

He shrugged awkwardly. Somehow this didn't seem the right time, but he could hardly deny it. "It's no big deal. Just part of a small show my agent set up."

"Just a small show?" Dori rolled her eyes. "He and Charlie Seeks Elk. Two of the best photographers in America."

"Charlie thinks it's a big deal," Milly added. "And so does the gallery. Poppy and I have been doing flowers for the food table. Classy and elegant, that's what they told us. There will be big people there. Critics. Art connoisseurs. Magazine writers. We'll all go en masse and brag that we're related to Deke."

"Of course we will," Carol said, smiling for real now. "That will be wonderful, Deke. I wish I'd known. I'll have to call Esther and Marilyn and—"

"Ma," Deke protested, embarrassed.

"Well, why not? It isn't every day my boy has a show right here in Livingston. I've only been to one, you know, that time Milly and I came down to Santa Fe, remember? But Dad's never been. He's only seen your books."

At least he'd looked at them. Or Deke hoped he had. He'd made it a point of sending them a copy of each of the five books he'd done.

"What's it about?" his mother asked.

It was hard to explain. You had to see the photos to appreciate his vision, to get a feel for his approach. Deke was an outdoor photographer. But he wasn't looking for calendar photos. Few of his shots could be called "pretty pictures."

He worked with space, with the horizon, with distance and perspective. His photos had a trademark expansiveness. They were always open, never closed. He went looking for places that gave him the opposite of the feelings he'd had when he'd stood in a building stamping prices on cereal boxes and sorting out brussels sprouts all day long.

He couldn't say that, of course. But because they were clearly waiting for him to say something, he had to try. "I went to the Four Corners area last winter, spent a week camping out in the snow, shooting a lot just at daybreak. Went over near Cortez and up on the mesas, looking down toward Shiprock. You know what it's like in winter before sunrise—all those muted colors, browns and taupes and grays—they can seem so flat, so dull. But then the sun comes up and the world seems to open up. All of a sudden there's coral and pink and rose, all these incredible possibilities…" He paused, feeling awkward at the enthusiasm that had crept into his voice.

He shrugged. "Anyway, it was…great." He took a breath. "And Gaby thought some of the shots I got would be a good balance for Charlie's work. She's been showing some of them recently at Sombra y Sol, her gallery in Santa Fe," he explained. And then he couldn't help adding the news he'd got right before he'd left, the news Gaby had been over the moon about. "They're going to be part of a show she's setting up this coming March in New York."

"New York!" his mother exclaimed. "Imagine that."

"And next summer they're going to be part of an exhibit in Cody called Wide Open Spaces."

"We'll have to get to that one," Riley said to Dori. "Don't think we'll make it to New York," he said ruefully.

"New York!" Carol murmured again. "That's wonderful. You've done so well, darling. Hasn't he, John?"

They all looked at him, even Deke. Especially Deke, who wanted just one tiny crumb of acknowledgment that he'd done better than he would have sorting brussels sprouts all day.

His father looked at him and said flatly, "I didn't ask to be impressed."

There was a second of stunned silence—as if all the

air had been sucked right out of the room. The mood deflated. The enthusiasm vanished.

Just like that. With a single sentence. Six words.

And if anyone had asked him minutes before, Deke would have said there were no words left with which his father could hurt him. They had, after all, flung so many at each other in their anger all those years ago.

But he'd have been wrong.

These hurt. They cut because they'd been delivered so deftly, so neatly, so unexpectedly, like a knife between his ribs, when Deke had merely been trying to explain himself.

He hadn't said it to brag, for God's sake, but to share his joy, to create a little understanding.

And he had been willfully misunderstood—and dismissed.

Deke pushed back his chair and stood.

Color high in her cheeks, his mother put out a hand. "Deke! Stay!"

But he shook his head. No one spoke as he removed the tray of Zack's high chair and scooped his son, midbite, up into his arms. "I have to go."

"But, Deke. There's pie."

He wasn't staying. Not even for pie. There was no point.

He'd come to make peace with his father. He'd come to put the past behind them, to meet his old man, one adult to another, to connect. He'd tried. Dear God, he'd tried.

They couldn't connect. His father refused. And Deke couldn't keep trying. It hurt too much.

He gave his mother, his sisters and brothers-in-law

and Jake a quick, thin smile, then bundled Zack into his jacket.

"Da!" Zack said, confused. "Pie?" He looked hopefully toward the table.

"No pie," Deke said.

"I'll put some on a plate for you," his mother offered, jumping up, coming after him toward the door.

"No. No, Ma." Deke did his best to smile at her, to try wordlessly to reassure her that this had nothing to do with her. "The dinner was fine. We're full. We don't need any pie." He opened the door and turned back to kiss her cheek and give her a squeeze. "It was good to see you."

She clung to him. "It was wonderful to see you, darling. We'll be there tomorrow night. Both of us. He doesn't mean—"

"He means," Deke said firmly.

"He doesn't think!"

Deke's mouth twisted. "I wouldn't know about that."

"He just says the wrong thing sometimes. He does love you, darling."

Deke just looked at her.

"We'll be there tomorrow," she vowed.

"It doesn't matter," Deke told her, giving her one more squeeze. "Take care of yourself, Ma." Over her shoulder he had a clear view through the living room into the dining room.

His father sat eating, eyes on his plate.

So much for burying the hatchet.

Another five minutes in his parents' house and he and his father might well have buried it in each other. He shouldn't have bothered to come. He wished to God he could leave right this minute and head back home. But he couldn't because, damn it all, he was stuck here until the show opened tomorrow night.

His fingers flexed on the steering wheel. What the hell else could go wrong?

It was snowing as he turned onto the highway toward Milly and Cash's place, and the truck skidded slightly. Instantly Deke slowed down.

"Pie?" Zack reminded him in a half plaintive, half hopeful voice.

"One-track mind?" Deke said, glancing wryly back at the little boy. Actually Zack had the right idea. If Deke had been focusing on important things—like pie—he'd be in a lot less danger of disappointment.

"We'll see what Aunt Milly's got at her place," he promised. "I think I saw her making some good stuff."

"Pie," Zack said happily and clapped his hands together, confident that his father wouldn't let him down.

Had he ever felt that way about his own father? Deke wondered.

Maybe. A long long time ago. He could, if he tried very hard, dredge up memories of his father ruffling his hair or laughing at one of his childish riddles or jokes. He remembered sharing a twin popsicle with his father on a hot summer day when they'd unloaded a truck at the back of the store.

When I was doing what he wanted me to do.

But by the time Deke was in college, they were barely speaking. There was no room in John Malone's life for a son who didn't follow the path he approved of. It was as if there was only one way to be a success— John's way.

When he'd left, Deke had been determined to do it his own way—and make his father proud of the man he had become.

Yeah, right.

Obviously he wasn't. *I didn't ask to be impressed.* The words still echoed, still stung, because it didn't matter to John Malone that his son was good at what he did. It didn't matter that Deke was—in the eyes of his colleagues, his critics and the world at large—a resounding success.

Because his father's approval had nothing to do with his success or lack of it, Deke realized. It had to do with the core of *who he was.*

And that, apparently, the old man disapproved of as heartily as ever. So he'd do them both a favor—this time when he left, it would be for good.

But—he rubbed a weary hand against the back of his neck—it wouldn't happen until after the gallery opening tomorrow night.

"Pie?" Zack said in a tone as weary as his fa-ther felt.

Deke shook himself and determinedly threw off the depression. What he couldn't change didn't matter.

"You want pie?" he said to Zack, who beamed at him. "I know where we can get you some pie."

And where he could have a good time, see some old friends and forget how stupid he'd been to hope that he and his father might ever see eye to eye again.

The main ranch house on the Jones place had been home to Will and Gaye Jones when Deke had worked there that summer nearly twenty years ago. It was where he'd gone after work on many cool evenings to sit on the porch and talk to Erin and, when he was home from rodeoing, her older brother, Taggart.

Deke knew from Milly that Will and Gaye had moved to Bozeman and Taggart, retired from bull riding with a world champion's gold buckle, had taken over running the ranch while he taught bull riding to young and not-so-young wanna-bes.

Looking at it now as he turned onto the road leading to the ranch house, he felt a quickening in his heart and soul, a feeling quite unlike the trepidation he'd experienced when he'd pulled up in front of his folks' place. The memory of his father's disapproval faded and he stepped on the accelerator.

Even with Erin halfway across the world, he was glad he'd come. He knew Taggart would be glad to see him. He could count on a warm welcome from Gaye and Will, who would surely be among the throng of dinner guests. There were more than a dozen trucks and cars parked haphazardly in the yard as he pulled up.

"Pie, Da?" came the voice from the back seat.

Deke glanced over his shoulder and grinned. "You betcha, sport. Coming right up."

As he opened the door to the truck he could hear the noise of laughter and the sound of happy people celebrating—giving thanks for the joy of each other. The way it ought to be.

"Hear that?" he said to Zack. "They're eating pie in there."

"Pie!"

A gorgeous blonde answered the door when Deke knocked.

Deke cleared his throat. "I'm Deke Malone. My sister—"

"Deke! Milly mentioned you last night. I'm Felicity, Taggart's wife. Come in and join the crowd."

She wasn't kidding about the "crowd." There were at least twenty-five people visible from where he stood—cowboys and kids, babies and women, old folks and young, toddlers and teenage girls and boys. Everyone was talking and laughing, balancing plates as they stood or sat on everything from sofas to steps to folding chairs. Some were eating turkey and cranberry sauce and mashed potatoes and dressing, others were already making headway into huge slices of pumpkin or apple pie.

Zack's eyes lit up. "Pie!"

Felicity laughed. "Want some pie, do you?" she asked him.

Zack stuck his thumb in his mouth and tucked his head against Deke's shoulder in a split second of shyness.

But when she said, "I think we can find you a piece," and continued to smile at him, he smiled back around the thumb in his mouth.

"This is Zack."

"Want some apple pie, Zack?" Felicity asked. "You look like an apple pie sort of boy."

Deke had just handed him over when he heard a voice behind him. "Deke Malone? Is that you?"

He turned to see Will Jones, white-haired now and more bow-legged than ever, but still lean and muscled, beaming at him. "Hey, Will!"

"By gum, if you aren't a sight for sore eyes, boy!" And Will wrapped him in a fierce bear hug—just as if Deke were his long-lost son.

Deke's eyes smarted and his throat tightened at the

real welcome he got here. He hugged Will fiercely in return. "Good to see you!"

"By heaven, boy, why didn't you say you were comin'?" Will stepped back and looked him up and down.

"It was spur of the moment," Deke said, which wasn't entirely true. "Milly's idea to get everyone here for Thanksgiving this year. On account of her C.J., and Dori's new baby. And they all wanted to meet Zack."

"Zack?"

Deke nodded just as Felicity returned with Zack and a plate of pie. She handed them both to Deke. "This is Zack."

Will's white brows hiked halfway up his forehead. He looked from Deke to the boy in his arms and back again, then grinned. "Well now, ain't he a chip off the old block." He ruffled the little boy's hair as Zack took a handful of pie and put it in his mouth.

Deke winced at the same time he felt a surge of pride. "I eat a little neater," he said with a rueful look at his son.

"Maybe now," Will allowed. "I do remember someone throwin' a few Rocky Mountain oysters at Taggart however."

He started it, Deke almost said. But instead he just flushed, grinning and shrugging.

Will took Deke's elbow and steered him through the crowded room.

"Look who's here!" he boomed as he hauled Deke into the kitchen. "Must be the year for prodigals!"

Everyone at the table looked up. A dark-haired man, a slew of kids, a gray-haired woman.

"Hey! You old son of a gun!" Taggart, the dark-haired

spitting image of his father, stood up, beaming. "Well, I'll be damned. It really must be old-home week!"

"Taggart, watch your language," said the gray-haired woman, whom Deke recognized as Gaye Jones.

The children looked at him blankly, though a pretty dark-haired girl about ten seemed to be grinning at Zack. Deke counted them—one, two, three, four, five, six. Taggart had *six* kids? Good God.

But suddenly he was distracted by a gasp of astonishment, and he turned to see a woman just turning around from taking a pie out of the oven. She, too, was staring—at him—her face flushed, her mouth open.

And Deke, equally dumbstruck, felt unexpected joy welling inside him as, grinning, he drank in the sight of her.

"Erin!"

Chapter 3

Erin? Here?

He couldn't believe it!

But even when he closed his eyes and opened them again—there she was, steaming pie in hand, staring at him in astonishment.

Grinning, Deke started toward her, eager to sweep her into his arms and give her a solid hug. But after two quick steps he stopped, realizing that with Zack in one arm and the pie plate in the other hugging was downright impossible.

Even so, it didn't stop him feeling a shaft of pure pleasure at the sight of her. She looked marvelous, slender still, but curvier than he remembered. She had breasts now—and hips. But she still had glorious long, dark hair and those gentle, expressive green eyes that he recalled so well.

The mere sight of her, even shell-shocked, made Deke feel much better.

"Better put the pie down before you drop it," Taggart suggested when the pie in Erin's hands wobbled precariously.

For a moment she still didn't move. Then suddenly she came to life, her mouth snapped shut and she turned quickly to set the steaming pie on top of the stove next to the two that were already cooling. She didn't immediately turn around, but instead stood staring down at the pie for so long that Deke had the worrisome thought that she might be trying to remember who he was!

"Erin?" he said. "It's, er, Deke. Deke Malone. Don't you remember me?"

She turned then, and she was smiling at him as she brushed her long dark hair away from her flushed face. "Of course I remember you. I was just surprised." She shook her head, disbelieving.

He knew how she felt. He couldn't stop grinning. "You and me both. I thought you were in Paris."

"I was. I thought you were in New Mexico."

"I was. I came for Thanksgiving. You, too?" Though even as he said it, he thought it seemed a long way to come for a four-day holiday.

"I live here now."

Deke's brows lifted in surprise. Why had Milly never told him? "At the ranch?"

"No. In Elmer."

"Elmer?" Which seemed almost stranger. "Since when?"

"We came in August and stayed at the ranch. Then

when Polly McMaster—you remember Polly O'Meara, who married Lew McMaster, who died…?"

"Yeah. She married Sloan Gallagher." Who didn't know the crazy wonderful story about Polly and Sloan and the cowboy auction that had taken place in Elmer earlier this year? It had hit every major paper and magazine in the world.

"She and her kids moved up to Sloan's ranch, and her sister married Jace Tucker and her mom married Walt Blasingame, so I bought their house."

Deke tried to process all the marriages. Mostly, though, he just smiled at Erin.

"And we moved in November first," she said. "Me and my kids." Her gaze went to the table, where the passel of kids were no longer paying attention to them, but were jabbering away.

"They aren't all Taggart's, then?"

Erin laughed. "He'd die at the thought. The oldest girl, Becky, and the youngest two, the twins, are Taggart's. The others—Gabriel, Sophie and Nicolas—are mine."

Deke looked over at the table and picked them out. The oldest boy, about twelve, he guessed, bore a startling resemblance to his mother—the same fine features, the same dark hair and green eyes that flashed as he argued some point with his cousin Becky. Though lean and wiry, too, the younger boy, who was probably about seven or eight, didn't resemble Erin at all, with his mop of strawberry-blond hair and faceful of freckles.

Sophie, with her long, brown hair and delicate features looked more like her mother. She reminded Deke of Erin in another way, too. She was quiet—

listening, watching—while both boys argued and chattered and laughed at the table now.

"I'd like to meet them," he said. He hesitated, then added, "I heard about what happened to your husband. Milly told me. I'm sorry."

Momentary pain flickered in Erin's eyes, and she smiled wistfully. "Thanks. I'm sorry too. He was a wonderful guy."

Deke was surprised by the pang he felt. Probably, he supposed, because he'd never considered Erin having affection for anyone but him. When he'd known her she'd never even had a boyfriend. She'd been *his* friend—always there whenever he'd wanted to talk or go riding or shoot photos.

Of course, obviously, she'd had a boyfriend later on—at least one: Jean-Yves LaChance. And she'd obviously felt affection for him because she'd married him.

But before he could think more about Erin's marriage, she brought him back to the present. "And who is this?" She was smiling at the little boy in his arms.

Deke felt the familiar swell of pride as he said, "This is Zack. This is my son."

Erin blinked. "Your son."

It wasn't quite a question, but there had certainly been an instant's hesitation in her words. And no wonder. Deke had told her often enough that he wasn't ever having kids. No way, he told her, was he going to put any kid through the misery his father had wished on him. Erin, ever sensible, had told him he shouldn't say such things, that he was far too young to decide, and that there was nothing that said he had to be the kind of father his own father had been.

Now Deke said, "You were right."

"Right?"

"I don't have to be my dad."

"Are we havin' that pie anytime this evening, Sis?" Taggart interrupted from across the room, raising his brows at her.

"Coming," Erin said hastily. She gave Deke a quick apologetic smile. "Must feed the clamoring hordes. You were lucky to get a piece of the first one." She nodded at the pie Zack had all over his face.

"Your dad gave it to him. Zack was in dire need of a piece of pie." And now he was in dire need of a washcloth. Both of them were becoming a sticky mess.

"Come sit down, Deke," her father called. "Gabe, shift over. Willy, pull up an extra chair for Deke. Becky, don't we have a high chair around somewhere?"

"In the closet. I'll get it." Taggart's older daughter jumped up.

"There now." Will beamed at Deke as the kids scrambled to do his bidding. "Come sit down and take a load off your feet. Bring that boy over here so we can get acquainted."

Torn, Deke looked from Will to Erin.

"Go on," she said. "Have a good visit. It was nice to see you again."

Nice? As if they'd been nothing more than casual acquaintances! Deke gave his head a quick, disbelieving shake. "What?"

"Dad's waiting," Erin said, sounding impatient.

"Okay. But I want to talk to you, too. To catch up, to find out what you're doing now. Meet your kids. Hell, Erin, it's been years!"

"I know how long it's been." She didn't look at him. She was cutting the pie and putting slices on plates.

"Deke!" Will commanded loudly.

"Coming!" he called over his shoulder, then turned back to Erin. "Later," he promised her. "I'm not leaving until we get a chance to talk." He gave her a wink, a conspiratorial grin and a light tug on a lock of her silky hair. "It'll be just like old times."

Just like old times?

Erin devoutly hoped not.

The last thing she wanted these days was to feel the aching desperation of unrequited love that she'd felt for Deke Malone for those five long years.

It didn't even bear thinking about!

It was certainly the last thing she'd been thinking about when she'd come to her brother's for Thanksgiving that afternoon.

Driving over the river and through the hills and trying to teach her French-born children to sing that old song, she'd been thinking to herself that, while the move to Elmer this past summer had been a good idea, it was very true that you "couldn't go home again."

And thank God for that. There was no way on earth Erin would have wanted to go back to being the sappy, passionate, awkward twenty-one-year-old she'd been when she'd last lived here.

She liked herself the way she was now—strong, independent, competent—a devoted mother and respected freelance magazine photographer, a capable adult woman who could manage alone.

Her parents said they understood that. They admired her independence, but recently her mother had taken to saying things like, "You may not always be alone, Erin. There will come a time when you'll be ready to look at men again."

And her sister-in-law, Felicity, Taggart's wife, had agreed. "*I* did," she said. And Erin, who had forgotten, remembered that Felicity had been a widow when Taggart had met her.

"Maybe," she'd allowed, because she didn't want to argue with them. But she didn't really believe it. As far as she could tell, her hormones had died when Jean-Yves had. Certainly they hadn't shown the least bit of interest in any man since.

Until now.

Deke Malone seemed to have brought them back from the dead.

And realizing it, all Erin could think was, oh, hell. Oh, hell. Oh, hell. Oh, hell. Because if there was one man on the face of the earth she did not want to start thinking about in that way again—if there was one man it was absolutely pointless to feel that way about ever—it was Deke!

She couldn't believe he was actually here!

When she'd considered moving from Paris back to Montana, the knowledge that she wouldn't be tripping over Deke Malone every time she turned around had been a big selling point.

Not, she'd assured herself at the time, because she'd still be in love with him even if he were, but because she didn't want to be constantly reminded of the foolish young girl she'd been.

Thank God Deke had never guessed.

In his eyes she'd always been a friend—his "best friend," he'd often told people. And whenever he'd said it, Deke would loop an arm over her shoulders and give her a squeeze.

Erin had lived for those moments of casual contact. She'd dreamed about them, embroidered them into the world's hottest fantasies—relatively speaking, of course. In those days she'd been pretty innocent in the ways of the world.

But remembering them now could still make her face flush.

She'd even hoped they'd go to Paris together, that they'd each get a fellowship. And that once there, no longer distracted by his long-standing battle with his father and the local girls who seemed all too willing to hop into his bed, Deke would discover how much he really loved her.

The stuff of foolish fantasies! Reality had been far different.

She'd got a fellowship and he hadn't.

"You can come, anyway," Erin had argued desperately. "You don't need a fellowship to go to Paris."

"Yeah, sure. Like I can afford to just pack up and move to Paris."

"You could," she'd insisted. "If you—"

"If I what?" Deke had challenged her.

But she couldn't say it, couldn't say anything, couldn't force him to dream her dreams. "Nothing," she'd said, trying to find a smile, to be his *friend*. "Never mind."

She'd blinked back tears and run out of the store. It was the last time she ever saw him. She'd been too busy, getting ready to leave to go down to Livingston, to say goodbye. *He* could have come to the ranch, she'd told herself. He could have changed his mind.

She'd dared hope that by leaving him alone he might just do that.

One more bit of foolishness.

"Aren't you going to call Deke and say goodbye?" her mother had asked her.

Erin had just shaken her head. "He's busy. I've got too much to do. I'll write him," she'd said.

She never had. She'd checked the post every day in hopes of finding a letter from him. But he didn't write, either.

I'll see him at Christmas, she'd assured herself.

But when she had come at Christmas, Deke was already gone.

"He and Dad had a big battle," Milly told her, "and Deke packed up and left. We don't know where he is."

She'd gone back to Paris, disappointed but determined to get over him. There was only so long even the most steadfast unrequited lover could hold out hope.

The following spring she'd begun dating a bit. She'd gone out a few times with a wildlife photographer named Nathan Wolfe and with a journalist, Trace Kennedy. But neither had made her heart beat faster the way Deke had.

She knew what he must have been feeling about her—Nathan and Trace had been friends, nothing more.

Then, several months later, it had happened. She'd met a young, intense photojournalist, Jean-Yves LaChance, who'd had the same intensity Deke had had.

Jean-Yves had asked her out. They had a wonderful time. They talked for hours over a bottle of wine. They walked the streets of Paris and ended up back at her place, talking all night. But there had been more than talking between them. Jean-Yves made it quite clear from the first that he didn't think of her as a "friend."

"I'll call you," he promised, even though he was leaving the next day for Morocco.

Erin hadn't expected to hear from him. But that night he rang. From Morocco. They'd talked for an hour. He'd called her every night while he was gone. When he came home, she met him at the airport. They spent every waking hour that she wasn't in school or he wasn't at work being together. And when he left for Lebanon and said, "I'll call," she believed him.

When he returned, Jean-Yves said, "Why are we spending money renting two flats?"

And Erin, unsure about living with someone—even the man she knew she loved, felt a nervous flutter. "Share one?" she said. "Live together?"

"Get married."

It had been perfect. "A marriage made in a darkroom," Jean-Yves jokingly said. But it was true—they understood and supported each other's work. He was delighted with her "human interest" pieces, and relieved that she was happy to be home with the family they soon started.

And she understood that the world's trouble spots were Jean-Yves LaChance's bread and butter. His need for adventure, for excitement, for shooting late-breaking news was simply part of who he was. And she knew it was risky. But it was a risk he needed to take.

"I'll be fine," he always reassured her, grinning that wonderful lopsided grin of his. "They don't call me LaChance for nothing." *The Lucky One, he meant.*

But then, on one fateful February evening, Jean-Yves LaChance's luck ran out.

He'd died instantly in cross fire between soldiers and snipers. He hadn't been the only journalist hit. Coincidentally, three days earlier Charlie Seeks Elk, who was now married to Cait Blasingame, whose family ranched a few miles away, had been shot as well. Charlie had survived.

Jean-Yves had not.

He'd been gone nearly three years. And while she could—and did—get by on her own, she still missed him. She didn't expect she'd ever look at another man, no matter what her mother or her sister-in-law had said.

She didn't want to look at Deke!

Her fingers gripping the knife trembled as she continued to cut the pie. Over the noise of laughter and chatter Erin could easily pick out his voice as he answered her father's questions. She couldn't tell what he was saying. She refused to strain to hear. She didn't want to hear. Didn't want to know.

Footsteps approached from behind her, and she tensed. But the voice was her brother's. "Pie, Erin? Anytime today would be nice."

"You're so desperate, cut it yourself," she said sharply.

"Whoa? What bit you?" Taggart raised his eyebrows.

"Nothing! I'm just…just tired." She'd been going to say *hot* and squelched that.

"Fine. I'll cut. Go sit down. Talk to Deke." He reached for the knife, but Erin jerked it away.

"No! I mean, no. I'll…do it." She raked a hand through her hair. "These are cut," she told him. "Put them on plates."

She tried to focus on the job at hand, tried to be the

calm, cool, collected woman she knew she could be, tried to be dispassionate about Deke.

But the truth was that the sight of Deke Malone, his head tipped back in laughter as he sat at the table between her son Gabriel and her father, affected her just as much as it ever had.

Time hadn't erased the awareness. It wasn't the surprise, the jolt, the unexpectedness of seeing him again.

It was the man.

Trust Deke Malone, she thought irritably, to improve with age. It wasn't fair.

At seventeen he'd been a handsome boy. At twenty-two he'd been a gorgeous guy—lean and well-muscled with fine strong features, thick dark hair and piercing blue eyes.

He was still lean, still as muscular as ever, but he was more solid. His shoulders were broader, his hair cut shorter and edged at the temples with a hint of gray. His face was a little less perfect. His nose looked to have been broken once or twice, and he had a scar by his left eye. There were grooves bracketing his mouth and tiny squint lines fanning out from his eyes that crinkled when he grinned.

Girls had always fallen all over him.

She wondered which one had finally settled him down.

Who had actually been more than his friend? Who had satisfied him body and soul and become the mother of his child? She couldn't help it. She wanted to meet this woman.

Deliberately Erin picked up two plates of pie and

carried them to the table. She set one in front of her father.

The second plate Erin held out to Deke. "I thought you might like one of your own." She felt pleased that none of her earlier agitation was evident. Her voice was warm and friendly, nothing more.

He glanced up and grinned that wonderful wicked grin. "Thanks."

Her heart skipped a beat. She'd obviously congratulated herself too soon. She took a deep breath. "So, where's your wife?" And then, because that sounded much too blunt, she added, "I'll bring another one for her."

Deke's smile turned a little wry. "No wife, I'm afraid."

"Oh. Sorry. I assumed—" she stopped and shrugged awkwardly, feeling equal parts cheered and dismayed by his reply. She hadn't thought he'd be divorced.

"Zack's mother died."

Even worse. Now she felt like an even bigger idiot. Deke had offered condolences to her about Jean-Yves and she hadn't even known his wife's name. "I'm so sorry. I didn't know. I didn't even know you were married."

"I wasn't." His mouth twisted. "One more thing for us to talk about."

Erin shook her head hastily. "No, no. That's not necessary. We don't have to—"

"We do," Deke said flatly. "Finding you here is the best thing that's happened." He smiled at her, and Erin felt traitorous melting feelings. Resisting them, she backed away.

"Hey, Deke," Taggart said as he passed around more

pieces. "You gotta come out to the barn and see our new stallion. Remember Shoeless? This guy's even better."

Deke's eyes lit up. "Love to see him."

Erin's traitorous feelings wanted to go see him, too—with Deke. She wiped damp hands on her jeans and backed right into a solid male body.

"Careful there." She turned to look into Cash Callahan's smiling face. He had a dusting of snow on his cowboy hat and he was still wearing his jacket.

"Oh, there you are!" Milly, with C.J. in her arms, swooped in on Deke. "We stopped at the house and you weren't there. Are you okay?"

"I'm fine," he said gruffly. "Don't fuss." He glanced around, caught Erin looking at him, and shrugged ruefully. "Same ol', same ol'."

"Your father? After all these years?"

He didn't answer, and that was answer enough.

"We were just going to take Deke out and show him the stallion." Will Jones pushed back his chair. "Want to come?" he asked Cash.

Cash beamed. "You bet. He's a beaut. You gotta see this horse."

"Show you the new bull riding arena, too," Taggart offered.

"Bull *and* bronc ridin'," Noah Tanner corrected, carrying a stack of dirty plates into the kitchen. He dumped them into the sink and snagged his jacket from the hook by the door. "It's pretty snazzy. Bleachers on one side. Just like the real thing. Let's go."

Deke took one last bite of his pie and got to his feet. He started to take Zack out of the high chair, but Will said, "Erin'll watch him. Come on."

Deke looked at her. "Would you mind?"

"No, of course not." She felt a mixture of emotions, but no, she didn't mind.

"Thanks." He winked at her, then reached out and ruffled his son's hair. "Be nice to Erin, buddy. She's my best friend in the whole world." Then he followed her brother and the others out the door.

In her dreams Erin had held Deke Malone's child in her arms. She had nuzzled her nose in his soft hair. She had kissed him and mopped him up and rocked him to sleep in her arms.

Tonight she did all these things.

It was lovely and bittersweet at the same time because he was Deke's son…but not hers. She sat in the corner of the sofa in the family room with the activity of a dozen kids and cowboys swirling around her, playing parlor games, laughing and arguing and teasing, while she cuddled Deke's sleeping son.

After Deke had gone off to the barn, she had supervised Zack as he demolished the rest of his pie. Then she'd carried him to the sink and washed his face and hands, despaired of the sticky apple all over his shirt and had sent Sophie to find one of Willy's outgrown ones.

Sophie, who adored babies, had helped change him, then took him to play with the other kids. There were easily a dozen-little Joneses, Nicholses, Tanners, Holts, Malones and McCalls, as well as some she didn't even know. But Zack had fit right in, playing happily until Hank McCall accidentally socked him in the nose with a tractor.

"Mama!" Sophie had snatched him up and brought him to Erin who had kissed his nose and rocked and soothed him while he rubbed his eyes and stuck his thumb in his mouth.

"Is he getting tired?" Sophie wondered.

To Erin's practiced eye, he had been. So she'd carried him over to the sofa and settled in, cuddling him and singing to him softly one of the songs she'd sung to her own children. Within minutes he had fallen sound asleep.

He still was, half an hour or so later, when Deke and Taggart came back inside.

"Oh, jeez." Deke hurried over when he spotted them on the sofa. "I'm sorry. Didn't mean to stick you with him."

"Not a problem." Except maybe a few twinges in the region of her heart. She rubbed her cheek against Zack's hair. "He was lovely. Just tired."

Deke flexed his shoulders. "It's been a long day." Erin thought he sounded even more drained than he looked. "I suppose I should get him back to Milly's."

Erin glanced at her watch. It was past ten. "And I need to get my kids home, too."

"We'll get together tomorrow."

"Sorry, I can't."

Deke's brows lifted, clearly surprised at being turned down.

"I'm busy tomorrow," Erin said quickly.

"All day?"

"Yes." Which wasn't precisely true, but while she'd been sitting there holding Zack, she had had time to think—and to make a decision.

It had been good to see Deke tonight. She was glad she had. But it would *not* be good to start daydreaming about him again. It would be unproductive and juvenile and she was far too old. If Jean-Yves had been alive, she wouldn't worry about it.

But Jean-Yves wasn't alive. There was, she realized, a hole in her life where Jean-Yves had been. And while she hadn't envisioned ever looking at another man again, she now realized that she might.

Tonight when she'd looked at Deke Malone again, she'd felt something she hadn't felt for a long, long time—interest, desire. You name it. Erin didn't want to.

And she didn't want to feel it, either—not for Deke. There was no point in feeling it when she knew it would never be returned.

"Tomorrow night—"

"Tomorrow night, too," she said. "I'm going to a gallery opening. Charlie Seeks Elk has an exhibit opening in Livingston."

Deke grinned. "At Dustin's? Me, too."

"You, too, what?" Erin said warily.

"It's my opening, too. Charlie's in the front room, I'm in the back."

Oh, hell.

"So, I'll see you there, right? We can go out after. Catch up."

Erin arched a brow. "Just like old times?" she said dryly. "You and me and Zack and Gabriel and Sophie and Nicolas?"

Deke made a wry face as he bent and scooped Zack out of her arms and settled the sleeping boy against his chest. "Well, maybe not exactly like old times." His gaze dropped to rest on Zack, then lifted again to meet hers. He winked. "I think they're better."

* * *

It was close to eleven when she and the kids finally left Taggart's place. The light snowfall that had begun about five had turned the landscape white and silent as Erin drove her Suburban back over the creek and down the winding road out of the foothills and into the valley toward Elmer and home.

In the back seat Nicolas was asleep and Sophie was yawning widely. Next to Erin in front, Gabriel was awake, staring out at the snowy landscape.

"Have a good time?" she asked. It had been their first American Thanksgiving, and Nicolas and Sophie had clearly enjoyed it, but with Gabriel, as quiet as the other two were noisy, it was sometimes hard to tell.

"Yeah." He slanted a glance her way. "I liked it. Were you worried?"

"Not really," Erin said, though she did sometimes wonder if the adjustment was harder for them than they led her to believe. "I just wondered. It's not exactly Paris."

"We always had Thanksgiving in Paris," he pointed out. And that much was true. Erin had always made sure that her children were aware of their American heritage. They knew all about the pilgrims and Squanto, the Declaration of Independence and the Fourth of July.

"Which wasn't exactly the same as here, though," she commented.

"Full of crazy cowboys, you mean?" Gabriel grinned.

She laughed. "It did get a little Western."

While Taggart and Deke and a few others were out in the barn, Felicity had organized the rest of the adults and teenagers into groups to play parlor games. Those who groaned about playing games ended up washing dishes. Between the silly charades and the outrageous guessing games and the bull riders and little kids who thought that snapping dish towels was the height of hilarity, things had turned just a little wild.

"It was cool," Gabriel said.

"Was," Sophie echoed from the back seat. "Liked that little boy," she murmured sleepily. "Didn't you?"

"Mmm. Yes." Erin didn't have to ask which little boy Sophie meant. If she bent her head she could still catch a whiff of the baby shampoo and apple pie smell that Zack had left on her sweater. Deke's child. The notion still made odd things happen in the pit of her stomach.

Deliberately she refocused, determined to think about something—anything—else. She needed to start thinking about her work. While she wasn't under serious financial pressure, she still needed something to fill her days. Several of the French magazines she'd done freelance work for had said she could contact them when she was ready. But she had held off, telling herself that they wouldn't be interested in photos from Montana. That was probably true—but it didn't excuse her from pursuing other markets. She hadn't, though. She'd been drifting since she'd come back to Elmer.

She wasn't even sure she wanted to do that sort of work anymore. Whenever she thought about it now, she felt hollow. She and Jean-Yves used to support each other's work. Now she had no one to share it with.

Polly McMaster had suggested that if she wanted to do something else, she could turn several of the bedrooms in their big old house into bed-and-breakfast rooms. "Get people who want a taste of the West," she'd said. "God knows Elmer's that. And it's got an international reputation now." She grinned now at the memory of The Great Montana Cowboy Auction they'd held last February that had put Elmer on the map.

"Maybe," Erin had said. And maybe she would. Certainly it was time to start thinking about doing something. She was restless suddenly. Fidgety. Tense.

Because Deke Malone had come back into her life.

He'd awakened her again as he had all those years ago. It had been Deke's advent into her teenage life that had given it color, excitement, promise. His work, his brains, his sensitivity, his gorgeous body—everything about him—had awakened her to possibilities she'd never considered.

She owed him the inspiration to follow her dreams, though he probably didn't know it. She owed him Jean-Yves and her children—and the best years of her life. Though he didn't know that, either, and would deny it if she told him, because he had never ever realized the effect he'd had on her.

And he would never know the effect that tonight he'd had on her again.

Sophie and Nicolas were both asleep by the time they got home. Erin woke them, then said to Gabriel, "I'll see these two upstairs. Sophie, Nicolas, come on. Let's go."

Sophie yawned. "Are we home already?"

"Yes. Nicolas, come on. I can't carry you." He was too big for that now. He leaned against her as she opened the back door and steered him in.

"I'll wake him up," Gabriel offered, a brotherly glint in his eye.

"I'll bet." And Erin could just imagine how. "No, thanks. You just deal with the dog. Nico! Stand up! Grandpa and Uncle Taggart have no use for lazy cowhands."

Bleary eyes opened. "'M I gonna be a cowhand?"

"If you can wake up in the dark," Erin said. "When Grandpa brings cattle in for branding, he gets up pretty early."

Nicolas straightened up promptly, and Erin aimed him toward the stairs. "No bath tonight," she said to Sophie, who was climbing the stairs ahead of them. "Just brush your teeth and head for bed."

She knew Nicolas wouldn't even get as far as the brushing teeth bit. He fell asleep on the bed again while she was taking off his boots. So she stripped him down to his underwear, tugged a pair of sweats on him, bundled him into his bed and kissed him good-night. He didn't stir.

When she went to Gabriel's room, he was just getting into bed. "I put Sammy out and I gave him some water."

"Thanks. I'm sure he appreciated it."

"He missed us. We should've taken him along."

"It would have just made things crazier."

Gabriel smothered a yawn. "Crazy is okay." He got into bed, settled against the pillow and looked up at her, his eyes assessing. "Are you okay?"

"I'm fine," Erin said quickly. "Why wouldn't I be?"

Gabriel shrugged. "I just thought…" He paused and considered things as he always did before he spoke. "Did you feel funny coming back for Thanksgiving?"

He was so sensitive to her moods. "It was different," Erin allowed. "It's been a long time."

"Yeah. I guess. I liked it. But after, I thought—" his midnight blue eyes met hers intently "—did it make Papa seem farther away?"

Erin felt her throat tighten. "Yes."

Gabriel swallowed. "For me, too. When we got home.

It was like…sad." His fingers twisted the edge of the comforter. "I miss him." His voice was so low she barely heard him.

Erin brushed a hand over his dark hair, then bent and kissed him. "Me, too," she said softly.

As one, they both looked at the picture on the table next to Gabriel's bed. It had been taken the last time Jean-Yves had been home, three weeks before his death. It had been a cold January in Paris, and they'd gone on a brief holiday to a small village on the Mediterranean. The first morning they were there Jean-Yves and Gabriel had rented a boat and gone sailing, just the two of them. And when they'd come home, sunburned and smiling, exhausted, but obviously well bonded and supremely content, Erin had snapped the picture of the two of them, Jean-Yves's arm around Gabriel's shoulders, as they strode up the walk.

Erin felt tears well now and prayed they wouldn't slide down her cheeks. She bit her lip.

Gabriel looked at the picture a long time. Then he rubbed a hand across his face. "He would have had a good time tonight," he said, his voice sounding rusty. He tried to smile at her.

Erin tried, too. Then she kissed him again. "Yes, he would have," she said firmly. Jean-Yves loved a good party. "And he'd be glad you did."

Gabriel nodded, the smile a little more real now. *"Oui."* He turned his head to look at the photo again. *"Bon nuit, Papa,"* he whispered. Then he turned to Erin again. "G'night, Mom."

Sophie was nearly asleep, but she opened her eyes when Erin entered. "It was wonderful, wasn't it?" she said sleepily. "All those people. 'Specially the cowboys. 'Specially Tuck."

Erin smiled. Sophie loved cowboys—especially red-headed, hazel-eyed Tuck McCall. Sophie had talked about Tuck ever since she'd noticed him last year. He was a lanky teenager now, a little awkward and sometimes shy, gifted artistically. He reminded Erin, personalitywise, of Deke. Fortunately he had a supportive family. If Tuck ever wanted to go to Paris to study, Erin was sure his uncle Jed and aunt Brenna would bust themselves to see that he got there.

"There were so many little kids, too," Sophie said. "Neile and Shannon and Hank and C.J. are going to be there tomorrow. Becky said I could come back and help baby-sit them."

"Would you like to do that?"

"Yeah. I like baby-sitting. Except for Nicolas." She wrinkled her nose. "He doesn't mind me. But the littler kids are fun. I liked Zack."

Erin hesitated, then smiled. "He was cute."

"I liked his dad, too."

"When did you talk to him?"

"I carried Zack's diaper bag out to his truck for him. He said I was a big help. He said I was just like you." Sophie was of an age where she still considered comparisons to her mother to be a compliment.

"That's nice," Erin said. Now it's time for you to go to sleep. Good night." She bent and kissed Sophie, then went to the door and shut off the light.

"Mama?"

Erin turned back. "What?"

"Do you ever think you might get married again?"

"What? No!" Where had that come from? She

went straight back to the bed and looked down at her daughter. "Why?"

Sophie wriggled in the bed. "Just wondered." She hesitated. Erin waited, knowing Sophie, knowing there would be more. "I was lookin' at Uncle Taggart tonight," her daughter said finally. "An' at Gus an' Noah an' Cash an' Mace an' Shane an' Jed." She plucked at the quilt, then shrugged silently.

"And?"

Another shrug. "I was thinkin' about havin' a father again."

"You're missing your papa?" Of course she was. Gabriel wasn't the only one sensitive to losing their father.

"I always miss him," Sophie said simply. "Every day. But I know he's not coming back. I mean a new father."

"Oh." Erin swallowed. Oh, dear. "Uncle Taggart does a lot of the stuff for you that fathers do."

"I know. But it isn't the same. It's better to have two parents."

"You've given this a lot of thought, have you?" Erin tried to smile and make things lighter than they were.

But Sophie nodded gravely. "Some. Me an' Becky talked about it. She only had Uncle Taggart until she got herself a mother."

"Do not," Erin warned, "consider matchmaking."

Sophie shook her head. "Matchmaking?"

"Finding me a husband."

Sophie yawned. "Already did."

"What?" Erin stared at her daughter, mouth open.

"Mr. Malone."

"Deke?"

Sophie nodded. "It makes sense. Zack doesn't have a

mother, and we don't have a father. You an' Mr. Malone used to know each other. He said so. That's better than Becky having to find Felicity for her dad."

Erin blinked at the workings of the ten-year-old mind.

"So, what do you think?" Sophie said seriously, as if she expected her mother to run right out and reserve the church. "Do you think it would work?"

"No," Erin said firmly. "I do not."

Chapter 4

Deke hated openings. He attended them because Gaby, his agent, would have had his hide if he didn't.

"Act like a grown-up," she always said. "Put on a tie. Smile. Say thank you. Drink club soda. And if you're going to wear boots, be sure they don't hurt."

So two or three times a year, whenever she hung a show for him, he put on a tie, drank ice water, said thank you, smiled till his jaw ached and forced himself to talk about his work. He was always cordial and polite and always desperately glad when it was over, because mostly it bored him silly. He liked taking the photos. He didn't care who came to look at them.

Except tonight.

Tonight virtually everybody who mattered in his life was going to be at Dustin's. His sisters and their husbands, his nephews and niece. His mother.

Not his father, of course. Deke had finally—last night, at long last—said goodbye to any lingering pipe dreams he'd had about a reconciliation with the old man. *It wasn't going to happen,* he told himself, *so get over it.*

And he would. He vowed he would.

So the old man didn't matter. But everyone else did. Besides his family, practically everyone else he knew in the valley seemed to plan on coming, too. A part of Deke wished he'd never asked Gaby to include him in the show. It was one thing to have a bunch of strangers who didn't matter look at his work and pass judgment. It was another thing entirely, he discovered, to care about what people thought.

He felt sick. What if they thought his work was crap?

What if *she* thought it was crap?

She. Erin.

Being judged by everyone else made him edgy. It made him chew on his thumbnail and crack his knuckles. It made him fumble as he knotted his tie. But it didn't make him sick to his stomach.

The thought of being judged and found wanting by Erin made him ill.

Last night he'd been thrilled to learn she was coming to the opening. He'd been that eager to see her again. And showing off his work had seemed like a good idea at the time. After all, it was through his first photos at Dusty's that she'd found him. She'd liked those, hadn't she?

But then she'd been sixteen, a girl—young and untutored. Now she was a professional. She was a woman. She had standards.

Deke just hoped he measured up.

And, oddly, not just on the photo front. Of course he

wanted her approval there. But all day long, every time
he'd thought about her—which was a lot—he hadn't
been thinking of her as a photographer, or even as his
old friend. He'd been aware of her as a woman. She'd
looked wonderful. More than wonderful. Gorgeous.

Deke had never thought of Erin as gorgeous.

Of course she'd always been pretty, with that long,
shiny dark hair and those big green eyes. If he'd thought
of her looks at all he'd thought in terms of words like
wholesome, genuine. Nice. She hadn't ever been the
sort of girl he'd had impure thoughts about.

He wouldn't have dared.

Hell, it would have been more than his life was worth
to put moves on Will Jones's daughter!

Besides, Erin had been his *friend.*

And that had been way better than a *girl*friend.

Deke had had more than enough girlfriends back
then. Tina, Gina, Sally, Susie, Holly, Lisa, Kelly, Lori,
Deb. He ticked them off in his mind, groping for their
names and finally giving up, sure there were more, but
unable to remember them all.

What he did remember was that they'd all simpered
and giggled and that their main claim to fame had been
their eagerness to put their hands all over him and, even
better, to let him put his hands all over them.

It had been damn enjoyable as far as it went. But even
as a lusty teenager Deke had known there was more to
life. Somehow he'd realized that he couldn't count on a
future in which he spent twenty hours a day with some
girl in the back seat of his dad's old Chevy.

And none of those girls had had much to offer
beyond that. What they'd wanted him to offer them
was a lifetime commitment and lots of money. And

they'd wanted him to give up his silly notion of making a career out of taking pictures. To a woman, they were on his father's side about that.

"What's wrong with the grocery store?" Tina had asked. "It's a steady income, isn't it? Your dad does okay." It didn't matter to her that Deke didn't want to do it.

"If you took pictures, you'd have to go places, wouldn't you?" Lisa had made a photographer's career sound like a terrible thing. She couldn't figure out why anyone would want to go anywhere.

Holly had said simply, "Taking pictures for a living? That's dumb."

Sally at least had liked the idea. "You can take pictures of me naked," she'd suggested, then, giggling, had run her hand down his chest to his belt buckle and beyond. "And I could take pictures of you," she'd added with a smile.

"They don't understand me at all," Deke had complained to Erin.

Erin had understood him completely. Erin had listened to him for hours. She'd sympathized, supported, teased, and when he'd needed it, had told him off.

When he told her what Sally had said, she'd rolled her eyes. "So become a monk. Stop dating. Become celibate."

He grinned now, thinking about that. As if!

But Erin had always had a way of cutting through the crap, of knowing what mattered.

He hoped when she saw his work tonight she wasn't disappointed. He hoped that when it came to deciding what mattered, she'd think he did.

"You ready yet?" Milly called through the bathroom door.

Deke took an extra swipe at his hair with the comb and straightened his tie one last time. Then he took a deep breath. "Ready." He opened the door. Zack toddled over and put up his arms. Deke picked him up. "Who's baby-sitting?"

"Susannah Tanner," Milly said. She came out of the kitchen with C.J. in her arms. "Her folks are dropping her off on their way to the gallery. You can go now. Cash and I'll come when she gets here. My, don't you clean up good?" She looked Deke up and down and whistled in amazement. "Is that a tie? I didn't know you owned a tie."

"The better to strangle you with, my dear," Deke said with a grin. He gave Zack a kiss and handed him to Milly. "Behave," he told his son. He started toward the door, all the butterflies in his stomach swarming madly.

"It'll be fine," Milly said to his back.

He hoped she was right.

Dustin's, the gallery where the show was being held, was a far cry from Gaby's Sol Y Sombra fine arts gallery in Santa Fe.

For one thing, it had only been Dustin's for the past year and a half. Before that, for at least thirty years, it had been Dusty's Art and Bait Shop—the art being photos of the biggest fish and elk and deer that local hunters bagged, the bait being what kept Dusty in business, along with the bit of taxidermy he did on the side.

But in recent years Livingston had undergone a bout of gentrification, and Dusty, Deke discovered, had attempted to keep up with the times. There were quite a few businesses in town that had. And there were new ones Deke hadn't seen before, like the Page and Leaf, a bookstore-cum-coffee-and-tea shop that would have looked right at home in Santa Fe, and a trendy, upscale restaurant called Sage's, the likes of which never would have survived in the Livingston Deke had grown up in.

There were still remnants of the old days, though. The pizza place he remembered as a boy was still where it had always been. And as he got out of his truck he was pleased to see that The Barrel, a rough-and-tumble cowboy bar, looked just as rough and tough and down-at-the-heels as ever.

Dusty's didn't. The old metal sign had been replaced by one made out of carved wood. And the decor no longer consisted of plaster walls covered with hunting and fishing shots, half a dozen stuffed ten-point bucks, one rather moth-eaten bear and Dusty's infamous busty-naked-women calendar on the back of the closet door.

In its new incarnation, Dustin's large front room sported high-tech track spotlights on recently finished wood-paneled walls, which were hung with collages made from fishing lures, arrowheads and driftwood, and amongst them were exquisite, tastefully framed photos of Montana wildlife—young antelope, deer, bear, beaver, otter and others—courtesy of Charlie Seeks Elk. Ferns hung in darkened corners, and a small waterfall trickled in an environmentally correct water-saving way over artfully arranged imported rocks.

Deke's own photos were hung in a room now called the Sundown Annex, which, if he remembered right, was where Dusty had done his taxidermy all those years ago.

Some things hadn't changed, though.

Dusty, for example, was still wearing his trademark red and black buffalo plaid shirt dressed up for the occasion by red suspenders and a red bow tie. He spotted Deke as he came in the door and hurried over. He was in his midseventies now, but what he'd lost in the quickness of his step and the hair on his head, he hadn't lost in enthusiasm or in the breadth of his welcoming gap-toothed grin.

"Deke, boy! By golly, look at you, all growed up!" He grabbed Deke in a bear hug that came near to cracking his ribs.

Feeling better at the enthusiastic reception, Deke hugged the old man back. "Hey, Dusty. Great to see you! Thanks for sayin' you'd show my stuff."

"Anytime! Reckoned you'da come back before now," the older man scolded. "Shoulda. Always got a place for you here. Told that agent of yours I put up your first show." He chuckled and snapped his suspenders. "Don't think she believed me."

Deke grinned because in fact Gaby hadn't. She'd called him after her first conversation with Dusty, reporting doubtfully, "I'm afraid this Dusty is a bit of a character. He claims to have 'discovered' you. Says he hung your first show."

Deke had explained about the elk hunt pictures and Gaby had been delighted. "Ah, well, that explains it then. No wonder he feels proprietary."

Now Dusty took Deke by the arm. "Come an' see how we cleaned the place up. Wantcha to meet my new partners." He drew Deke toward the refreshment table set up along one wall between the two rooms

Marjorie and Hal Goodnight, the new partners,

were a bit younger than Dusty and considerably more conventionally dressed. They shook hands and offered him a glass of wine and the usual platitudes. Deke would have liked the wine to settle his nerves, but opted for ice water instead. He practiced smiling. More people were coming in. He spotted Brenna and Jed McCall just inside the door.

"Better check on Charlie. See if he needs anything," Hal said, and drifted away.

Marjorie went on speaking knowledgeably about Deke's photos and even making comments on a couple of his books, and Deke forced himself to pay attention, but his gaze kept wandering toward the door. He wondered when Erin would come.

"Have you met Charlie Seeks Elk?" Marjorie asked eventually, nodding toward the front of the gallery where several people were gathered around a series of photos. Charlie's blue-black hair glinted in the lights.

Deke nodded. "Met him in Santa Fe a few years back. It's pretty amazing to change focus the way he has."

When Deke had met him, Charlie Seeks Elk had been a photojournalist with an international reputation. He'd spent the early years of his career shooting gritty urban America, and then had moved on to war zones in various parts of the world. His articles and books had shown life at its most desperate and hopeless. They had been calls to action, to compassion, to concern.

Then three years ago Charlie had been shot. He'd been wounded critically. Gaby said he'd coded—had been clinically dead. Somehow, though, he'd battled his way back to life.

When he'd left the hospital, he'd come to Montana to recuperate, to regain his health and his focus—and to find Cait Blasingame. Since then his work had taken an entirely different slant. His latest book, *Morning Has Broken,* focused on children—human and animal. It drew connections. It spoke of hope.

Now Deke moved to study Charlie's photos, determined to take his mind off worrying about when Erin would show up—and what she'd think when she did. Charlie was every bit as good at this as he had been at his earlier work. He still had an eye for a story—it was only the story that was different.

Three years ago Deke's work—his silent canyons, vast empty skies and stark barren landscapes—would have seemed grand and inspiring compared to Charlie's harsh gritty, tightly focused images.

Now their roles were reversed. Charlie's new work was more accessible and less lonely and remote than his.

"Oh, there you are, Deke!" Gaye Jones came bustling up and threw her arms around him. "Don't you look nice." She touched his tie. No one who used to know him, apparently, believed he owned a tie. "What a wonderful turnout. And your work—it's stunning. We've been bragging about knowing you. Come meet our friends."

Deke turned to see Will approaching with a small mob of people trailing in his wake. He did a double take. "What'd you do, bring half of Bozeman?"

Will clapped him on the back. "Had to prove to these folks that I knew you. They didn't believe you used to work for me."

Deke laughed. "Didn't you tell them you taught me everything I know? It's true," he told Will and Gaye's friends. And then, with Will asking leading questions, he found his stride and began to talk about the photos behind him.

It got easier after that. A steady stream of people kept coming. Brenna McCall, an accomplished artist in her own right, said all the right things and made him feel even more at ease. Then Taggart and Felicity appeared, along with Becky and a tall, lanky boy with thick rust-colored hair who turned out to be Tuck McCall.

The Nicholses showed up. So did the Holts, along with Jace and Celie Tucker and Artie Gilliam.

Artie, who had already been an old man when Deke left, had to be on the far side of ninety now. He was moving slowly but he studied each picture intently before moving on. When he reached Deke, he held out his hand. "Don't get around like I used to," he said, shaking Deke's hand. "Can't barely get up and down the steps these days. So seein' these is like takin' a trip again." He smiled and gripped Deke's hand even harder. "Thanks."

"You're welcome. Thank *you*." Before he could say more than that, Deke found himself overrun by his sisters, their husbands and Jake.

"Wonderful," Milly said.

"Stunning," Dori agreed.

"Wow," Cash said, while Riley just stood and nodded his head.

"Hi, Uncle Deke. These are cool." Jake was bouncing up and down on his toes. "I wasn't sure I wanted to come on account of it might be boring. But Charlie's got some amazing pictures of bears. An' I like these horses in the canyon." He tipped his head toward a panoramic photo of a herd of running mustangs that

Deke had taken from the top of a mesa. "It's like bein' there. Lots better'n in books."

"High praise," Riley said in case Deke didn't realize it.

Deke did. He grinned, bounced a little in his own boots, butterflies settling.

And then, through the crowd, he saw Erin.

She was halfway down the long gallery talking to Charlie, nodding at one of his photos. And Charlie was nodding, too, then pointing something out, then laughing at whatever Erin said.

Deke, watching, couldn't get over how elegant she looked. The wholesome country girl he remembered had turned into a cultured cosmopolitan woman. She wore a sleeveless black dress of the less-is-more variety, very short, very stark, very very sexy.

If it was hard to think of her as the girl he'd known, it was equally hard to think of her as the mother of three young children. In her elegant dress, with her feet in heels and her hair piled high on her head, she looked like the epitome of Parisian sophistication. She dimpled now, smiling at something Charlie was saying. Then she put her hand on Charlie's sleeve, took her farewell and headed straight for him.

Deke swallowed, then took a quick gulp from the glass of water he was holding and watched her approach. He felt as if he was caught in her sights. There was no way on earth he could look away.

She was smiling by the time she got to him, looking cool and classy. "Deke," she said, and leaned forward, giving him air kisses and the brush of her cheek against his in quintessential European fashion.

He cleared his throat and smiled at her when she stepped back. "Hey. You came."

"Of course. I told you I was coming. What a great turnout."

"They're here for Charlie. Just like you are." He reminded her of what she'd said last night.

"You're going to hold that against me forever, aren't you?" But she was smiling as she said it. "I hadn't heard you were going to be here, too. I'm not in the Livingston art loop, I'm afraid. Obviously a lot of people did know." She nodded at the crowd milling around. "They're here for both of you. You've done well. I see some stickers."

There were bright blue circles indicating sales in the bottom right-hand corner of several of his photos.

"My sisters probably," Deke said.

Erin shook her head. "I bought the Canyon de Chelly one."

"You did? Why did you do that? Hell, I'd have given it to you."

"I bought it because I like it. It...speaks to me." The photo was of a young Navajo shepherd boy with a flock of sheep. They were dwarfed by the red rock canyon walls, but the boy was looking up and there was a single narrow strip of blue sky above. "All your photos have sky," Erin said, having discovered what few others had. "But this one had hope, this boy had dreams. This picture had it all."

She smiled at him, and Deke stared at her, dazed. It was as if she'd seen right into the heart of him exactly the way she used to. It was as if the past fifteen years hadn't intervened at all.

"Deke!" Milly appeared behind Erin's shoulder, looking agitated, waving her fingers at him. "Deke!"

He tore his gaze away from Erin. "What? What do you want?" He didn't want to talk to anybody else, didn't want to see anybody else, didn't want to bother.

"Mom's here," Milly said. "Dad's with her!"

And Deke felt his stomach do a triple somersault. All those hopes he'd banished came rushing back. All his dreams of reconciliation, of making his father proud, of the two of them finally coming to terms once more filled his head.

Erin reached out and patted his arm. "Go on," she said. "It's your night. Go see him."

"But—"

But Erin melted away into the crowd of folks her parents had brought with them from Bozeman, and Deke was left standing there watching his parents work their way up the length of the room. Of course they had to look at Charlie's photos. It was first and foremost Charlie's show—and of course the Malones were unfailingly polite.

So Deke clenched his water glass and waited. Held his breath as he watched. His father didn't look happy to be there. He looked, in fact, as though he were in pain.

He was staring distractedly at one of Charlie's photos of some bears fishing in a stream while his wife talked to Charlie's wife, Cait.

Milly tugged Deke's hand. "Come and talk to him."

But Deke couldn't. "Let him look. I'm not goin' anywhere."

"Stubborn cuss." Milly shook her head.

"I'll be here," Deke said firmly, his fingers strangling the water glass, wishing it were something else. Straight whiskey wouldn't have gone amiss right now.

"Oh, Deke! Here you are!" His mother, spotting

him, flew at him. "Isn't this wonderful? The photos are stunning. And all these people!"

"Uh-huh," he said, distracted, watching his father over her head. The old man was standing quite still now, staring at the wall. "Glad you got here."

"I'm sorry we're late. John was working—"

"I'm surprised he's here."

"Of course he came." She glanced back toward her husband. Will Jones was talking to him now, pointing out Deke's photos, slinging his arm over John Malone's shoulder and guiding him from one to the next.

Deke tried to gauge his father's reactions and listen to his mother's cheerful comments at the same time. She was effusive. His father's jaw was clenched. Was that sweat beading his upper lip?

Cripes, was he going to have an anxiety attack just because he'd had to come to a gallery reception for his son? Deke wondered.

Will took him all the way around the annex, making sure Deke's father got a good look at every picture. Then Deke heard him say, "Come on over and sit a spell. Reckon Deke will want to talk to you about them."

John Malone shook his head. "Can't. Got to get back to work." And leaving Will Jones standing there, he turned toward the door. "Can't stand around here wasting a whole evening. Shelves don't stock themselves," he said flatly.

Deke didn't move, just stared as his father walked stiffly past him. A hand slid into his and squeezed gently.

Erin was there beside him, wrapping her fingers around his as, gutted once more, he watched his old man go.

* * *

The trouble with muscle memory was that it worked. You did the things you'd always done without even thinking about them. Like watching Deke out of the corner of her eye, always being aware of where he was, who he was with, what he was feeling.

Even after fifteen years the habit was still there. And when Erin saw him go still as he watched his father's slow progress around the annex, even though she'd backed off, she found herself edging close again. So that she was right behind him, close enough to reach out and take his cold hand in hers as he'd stood, stricken, and watched his father turn without speaking to him and walk away.

She didn't even realize she'd done it. It had been automatic. Even more automatic than the self-preservation that had had her deliberately putting on her most sophisticated Parisian dress, like it was battle armor, before she'd come this evening.

Fat lot of good it had done her. She'd walked in, prepared and determined to be indifferent to his drop-dead gorgeous self—even in coat and tie—only to be blindsided by his photos instead.

She had his books. She knew his work. He'd become every bit as insightful as she'd once imagined he would. On the page his photographs were interesting; on the wall they overpowered her. They drew her in, simply grabbed her by the throat and thrust her into the world according to Deke Malone.

It was a stark world, a vast world—but it didn't daunt so much as it offered possibilities. That's what she'd seen in the photo of the young Indian boy and his sheep. He was caring for them, but he wasn't consumed by them. His eyes were on the sky—on the limitless sky overhead.

She had told herself she could resist Deke in the flesh, but she couldn't resist that photo. It reminded her of Deke himself—the boy he'd been, the hopes he'd had. And here tonight she saw them realized. She'd found Marjorie and bought the photo before she did anything else. Having bought it, she thought, she would settle down. She would know that when Deke left, a piece of him would stay with her. She would have it as she would never have him. She'd even managed to rationalize that.

But now she had to rationalize the fact that she was holding his hand.

He was a friend, she told herself. He'd always be a friend, no matter what. She hated seeing him hurt. Hated the way his father had once more rejected him, hated seeing the bleak look in his eyes. She wanted to ease the pain, make it go away.

And muscle memory affected her mouth, too, for she suddenly found herself saying, "Come back to my place."

Deke looked around and seemed almost surprised to see her there. His expression changed from bleak to confused to something she couldn't quite read.

"You don't have to, of course," she said quickly, self-preservation kicking in at last. "I just thought…"

"I want to," Deke said, his voice low and ragged. A muscle in his temple throbbed. He was crushing her hand. He glanced at his watch. "It's 9:30. Let's go." He looked as if he would bolt right now if she didn't stop him.

"Not yet," Erin said. "You need to stay till the end. And I came with Taggart and Felicity. I'll go home with

them, and you can meet me there." It would give her a
chance to get her defenses in place again.

"Deke?" Marjorie Goodnight tapped him on the
shoulder. "There's a reporter here from the *Chronicle*.
Could you speak to him?"

Deke hesitated, but Erin nodded encouragingly and
eased her hand out from his. "Go on. Come when you're
finished. The big two-story white house on the corner
as you come into town."

Deke still frowned, then sighed and nodded and
actually managed a smile for Marjorie and the reporter.
But he caught Erin's hand as she turned to go. "Leave
the light on for me."

Chapter 5

Casual, Erin told herself. Offhand. Unflustered.

She had to treat him exactly the way she'd treated him years ago. Like her buddy. Like he was a pal. A good old friend and nothing more.

"Are you going to get out of the car or did you want to come home with us?" Taggart's voice, just a little impatient, jerked Erin back to the present—and the reality that they were sitting in the middle of the main road through Elmer directly outside her house.

"Oh! Sorry! I was just…thinking." About Deke, about spending time with him again—the one thing she'd tried to avoid, and she'd been the one to suggest it! Now she opened the door and scrambled out. "Thanks for the lift. Um, do you still want Gabriel in the morning?"

"I said I did." Taggart shook his head at her scattered thoughts. "Dazed and confused, are we?"

"She's just excited. It was a great opening. And she ran into so many people tonight that she hasn't seen in a long time," Felicity offered as an excuse for Erin's rude behavior.

"I didn't see her talking to anyone but Deke," Taggart said.

His wife grinned. "All the more reason she can't be expected to pay attention to you."

"Thanks very much," Taggart said dryly.

Felicity looked at Erin. "I do like him, Erin."

"Like who?" Taggart said blankly.

Erin didn't say, Like who? She knew.

"It's not like that," she protested. "We're old friends, that's all."

"Who's old friends?" Then the penny dropped, and Taggart laughed. "You mean Erin and Deke? Together?" He was grinning all over his face now. "That's a good one!"

"See?" Erin said to her sister-in-law. "He knows."

"Taggart knows? About men and women?" Now it was Felicity's turn to laugh. "Color him clueless."

"Now wait a sec," Taggart said, offended.

"Ask Becky if you don't believe me," Felicity reminded him.

"That little manipulator," Taggart grumbled. Then he shot his wife a knowing look. "But she didn't just nail me. She nailed you, too."

"Smarter than both of us," Felicity agreed, unperturbed, then she glanced back at Erin. "Want me to send Becky around to help you out with Mr. Malone?"

"No, I don't!" Erin said forcefully. "Good night. Thank you for the ride. Go home now, Taggart, and do something interesting that will keep your wife busy."

"Something interesting?" Taggart said speculatively. "Now there's an idea." He grinned broadly and waggled his eyebrows in Felicity's direction. "Come on, wife. Let's see what we can find to keep us busy."

Laughing and shaking her head, knowing exactly what her brother had in mind, Erin shut the car door and waved them on their way. Then she made her way up the walk and climbed the steps.

The house still seemed huge. Of course, they'd only been living in it a month, hadn't really had a chance to fill it up yet. But with six bedrooms, two baths, a double parlor, eat-in kitchen, mud room and sunroom, it was easily four times bigger than their flat in Paris.

She hung up her coat, kicked off her heels and actually had to go looking for Gabriel, who had been deputized to baby-sit his siblings for the evening. She found him in the sunroom, watching a video.

"Everything go okay?" she asked, wriggling her toes gratefully.

"*Oui.* Yes. Mostly." Gabriel shrugged his shoulders against the back of the couch, then hit pause on the remote and looked up at her. "Nico didn't want to take a bath. He said I couldn't make him. He was wrong."

"I see," Erin said, sure that she did. "Is the bathroom still standing?"

"Uh-huh. But we're pretty much outa towels."

Not as bad as it might have been, then. "We'll do laundry in the morning. What are you watching?"

Her children had had their pick of almost-current

videos because Celie Tucker ran her C&S Spa and Video out of the shop on the back of the house.

"Raiders," Gabriel said happily, which wasn't current at all. He punched the remote and settled back to watch his favorite film. This wasn't even Celie's video, but their own, one that Gabriel and Jean-Yves had watched over and over.

Was he still missing his father? Erin wondered. Or was he watching it merely because he liked it?

The film was a little more than halfway over, and Erin would have liked to suggest he finish it tomorrow. But it was understood that on nights he baby-sat for Sophie and Nicolas, Gabriel was entitled to a later bedtime. She could hardly expect to shoo him off to bed just because she had invited company home. He would wonder what was going on.

And the truth was, *nothing* was going on.

It wasn't as if she was planning a big seduction. Deke was coming over, and they were going to talk, just as they had always talked. Nothing was going to happen, because nothing ever happened.

And that was fine with her.

Still she found herself saying casually, "It's nearly eleven. Maybe you should finish watching that tomorrow night. Uncle Taggart will be here to pick you up early."

"I'll be ready," Gabriel said, his gaze on the screen.

Erin shrugged. "Whatever. I'm going up and changing out of this dress." She started up the stairs, wondering if she should say anything about Deke coming by or not. No wonder she never invited men home. It was too difficult. There were too many decisions.

"Want some popcorn?" Gabriel asked.

Erin hesitated, then shrugged. "Sure. Why not?"

She went upstairs and took off the basic black dress, then unpinned her hair and shook it loose. It was always possible that Deke might change his mind and not come. But if he did, she didn't think she should be entertaining him in her nightgown. So she put on a pair of jeans and a forest-green cashmere sweater, stuffed her feet into a pair of moccasins and went back down.

The movie was on pause and Gabriel was in the kitchen making popcorn in the microwave. When she appeared, he looked her up and down, surprised.

"Deke Malone might be dropping by," Erin explained offhandedly, getting down a bowl for the popcorn. "He's the guy whose opening I went to tonight." In case he didn't remember.

Gabriel didn't say anything. Sophie would have asked ten questions by now.

"We're old friends," Erin said, thinking as she did so that Gabriel probably found out more by *not* asking than Sophie did by giving her the third degree. "We haven't seen each other in years, and we decided we had a little catching up to do before he heads back to New Mexico." That sounded like a reasonable explanation.

Gabriel took the popcorn out of the microwave.

"He used to work for Grandpa when we were in high school and college. I've known him a long time." Erin kept on.

It didn't matter to Gabriel. He split open the popcorn bag and dumped it into the bowl, then carried it back into the sunroom. Shutting her mouth before she said something she'd really regret, Erin followed and sat next to him on the sofa.

Indiana Jones was in the well of souls surrounded by snakes, his life at stake. Erin tried to focus on his dilemma. It wasn't easy.

And it got harder minutes later when there was a knock on the door just as the Nazis were shutting Indy in. She jerked and almost spilled the popcorn.

"Sorry!" She thrust the bowl into Gabriel's lap and scrambled to her feet. Then she stopped and made herself take a deep breath.

Cool it, she commanded silently. *It's only Deke. It's no big deal.*

Certainly, she reminded herself, it wasn't to him. Keep that in mind, she told herself, wiping damp, salty palms on the sides of her jeans as she went to open the door.

Deke had changed clothes, too. The coat and tie were gone. So were the dark wool slacks. He was wearing faded blue jeans and a black watch plaid flannel shirt beneath a forest green down jacket. Flakes of new snow dusted his black cowboy hat.

"Hey." He smiled at her, but the smile was forced and didn't quite reach his eyes.

Erin knew why, and knew she wanted to help, knew she could help because this was Deke—and she always had helped him. She felt adult, in control and sensible again. "Hey, yourself," she said, smiling as she opened the door wider. "Come on in."

He came in. "I stopped at Milly's to check on Zack. Figured I'd bring him if he was awake and causing trouble, but he was asleep so Milly said to leave him. So I shouldn't stay long. Don't want to stick her with my responsibility, but—" he looked her square in the eyes "—I wanted to come."

She hung his jacket over the newel post and dropped his hat on the bench beside the door. Deke pulled off his boots so he didn't track snow into the living room, then straightened up once more. In his socks he was only three or four inches taller than she was. Her eyes were on a level with his mouth. She turned away quickly.

"We can sit in the living room or the kitchen or—" she said as she led him into the living room. Gabriel still had the video on in the sunroom. The sound carried faintly this far.

Deke stopped. "Is that *Raiders?*"

"What?" Erin glanced back at him, baffled, then realized he was hearing the theme music from the movie. "Gabriel is watching it."

This time Deke's grin was real. "Can we?"

Erin almost laughed. "Of course."

If Gabriel was surprised to have company, he betrayed it only by the barest widening of his eyes when they both came into the room and sat with him on the sofa.

"Ah, great. My favorite part," Deke said with relish as Indy struggled to cling to the bottom of the truck carrying the Ark. "Taggart and I used to spend hours trying to figure out how we could do that."

Gabriel looked impressed. "Did you do it?"

"I bet you can't get this whole bowl of popcorn in your mouth all at once," Erin said pointedly to Deke. The last thing she needed was him giving Gabriel ideas like that.

But he just laughed. "No," he said to Gabriel. "Your grandfather told us that if we ever wrecked one of his trucks pulling some damn fool stunt, he'd blister whatever was left of our hides." He winked at Erin, then looked at the bowl on the table in front of her. "Pass that popcorn, will you?"

They watched the movie, the three of them, until the end when bureaucracy overtook and stultified adventure and scientific pursuit.

"That part," Deke said, stretching his arms over his head, "is only a joke if you haven't lived it." His smile was wry and sad.

And Erin knew that however welcome the respite of losing himself in the film had been, the ending had brought back the conflict with his father. "Come along now," she said to Gabriel. "Bedtime."

"I've got the stunt video," Gabriel said eagerly to Deke, "where they show you how they did stuff. My dad and I used to watch it all the time. It's cool. If you want we could—"

"Gabriel!" Erin arched her brows at him.

"But—"

She tapped her watch. "You've seen the movie. It's time for bed. Now."

His shoulders slumped, and Erin felt the tiniest bit guilty because she sensed that his eagerness was not feigned merely to get to stay up longer, but because he'd found a kindred spirit in Deke Malone.

"Another time, perhaps," she said firmly, though she knew there wouldn't be any other times. Deke would be heading back to New Mexico tomorrow.

"Uh-huh." Gabriel's tone told her he knew that, too. He rewound the tape, then put it in the box and kissed her good-night, then glanced at Deke. "Good night."

As soon as he'd gone upstairs and they were alone, Erin felt pricklings of awareness that made her want to call him back. "Coffee? A glass of wine? A beer?" she asked.

Deke raised a brow. "Wine? In Elmer, Montana?" As if it were unheard of.

Erin laughed. "Well, I snuck some in. Too many years in Paris. Forgive me."

"Actually," Deke said, "I wouldn't mind a glass of wine." And at her lifted brow he grinned and added a little wryly. "Too many years in Santa Fe."

Erin led the way into the kitchen. She offered him a choice of the bottles she'd brought with her from France. He looked them over, nodded appreciatively and chose the cabernet. When she got out a corkscrew, Deke took it and opened the bottle with practiced ease while she fetched glasses.

"Times change," she said, watching him. "You couldn't have done that fifteen years ago."

"I couldn't have afforded wine that came in a bottle with a cork in those days, anyway."

"Or been old enough to drink it—legally."

"That, too." He handed her one of the glasses and raised the other in a toast. "To the years."

"And the miles," Erin added, echoing Indiana Jones.

"And the friends," Deke added.

Their glasses clinked. Their eyes locked. And Erin, in danger of drowning in the deep blue of his gaze, took a hasty gulp and nearly choked on it.

"All those years in France," Deke murmured, shaking his head as, eyes watering, Erin coughed and cleared her throat.

Embarrassed, Erin could do nothing but laugh at herself.

"So tell me," she said, when she could manage to

speak again, "about those years in Santa Fe. Come in, sit down and tell me about your life." Carrying her glass and the bottle, she led the way into the living room.

"Want a fire?" Deke nodded toward the living room fireplace.

"Oh, yes." She didn't take the time to build one often herself, but she loved them. A fire in the fireplace always made a house seem cozier, homier. Having a fireplace was one of the things she'd missed in their flat in Paris.

Now she watched as Deke built the fire with the same efficiency he'd shown with the bottle of wine. Then, when he had it going to his satisfaction, he stepped back, picked up his glass and came to join her on the sofa.

"Your life," Erin prompted, swallowing carefully as he sat down. He'd turned sideways to face her and his knee very nearly brushed her own. Unbidden, the traitorous pounding of her heart kicked up a notch.

"All fifteen years in a nutshell?" Deke said a little wryly. But at her nod, he thought a moment, then began. "I left a little while after you did. Had a bust-up with my dad that you weren't here to help me think my way out of. So I figured it was time to get out. But I couldn't afford to go to Paris, so I just went west." He swirled the wine in his glass reflectively, then stared into the fire and went on. "I worked on half a dozen ranches, earned enough to buy film and get it developed, and when I could afford to send photos out to magazines, that's what I did. I sold a few. Barely enough to keep the wolf from the door of my truck, which is what I was living in at the time."

At the sound of Erin sucking in her breath, he said

quickly, "It wasn't as bad as it sounds. It worked out fine. I didn't have any money, but I didn't feel poor. I bummed around most of the West for a year getting nowhere, and then I decided maybe I'd make my fortune riding broncs."

"You?" Erin was amazed. Deke had never had the rodeo bug.

"Me. And that turned out to be a worse idea. I broke my arm in Salinas about two weeks out, and that ended my rodeo career right there. Worst of all, I couldn't hold a camera for about six weeks. Lucky for me, I'd sent off some slides to Enrique Castillo—"

"*The* Enrique Castillo?" Enrique Castillo had been a mover and shaker in the art world, in photography and other media, for many years. He was so well-known that even in Paris she'd heard of him.

Deke nodded. "Luck of the Irish, I guess. I was still laid up when he tracked me down. He took one look at me with my arm in plaster and my stomach growling, and said, 'You're an idiot. You do what you're not good at. It will break you in little pieces. Come to Santa Fe.'"

"Just like that?"

Deke smiled reminiscently. "Just like that. And I told him I couldn't afford to. And he said, 'You can't afford not to. If you don't take your work seriously, who will?' And then he walked out. I had a lot of time to think. And I decided he was right. So I went to Santa Fe. It took me two months, but I got there. He found me a place to live, gave me a job in his gallery, taught me the sales angle and the business angle and told me to keep my eyes and ears open and learn. I sold pictures. I swept floors. I did the accounting." He grimaced. "It was like the damn grocery store all over again. But at the same time he taught me how to present my work. I matted and framed photos, and I got to listen to every photographer and artist who came through. It was an education and a half. It was incredible. I learned."

Erin, marveling at his tale, sat back and grinned. "That's fantastic. Truly. And I feel vindicated," she added. "I told you that you had talent."

"Yeah, well, you were the only one who could see it back then."

"You saw it."

"But I didn't really trust it."

"Do we ever completely trust our own instincts?" Erin could think of plenty of times she'd *hoped* something was true, but it hadn't always worked out. Deke and herself together, for example.

"Probably not." Deke sighed and shifted on the sofa, leaning back and stretching his long jeans-clad legs out in front of him. There was, Erin noted, a hole in the toe of his sock. She let her gaze slide slowly up the denim, then, realizing what she was doing, shifted her gaze quickly away to stare into the fire. It seemed a less dangerous object of contemplation.

"What about you?" he asked.

So she told him about her life in Paris, about what a wonderful opportunity to grow and learn she'd had at the institute, how it had helped her develop as a photographer, how she had discovered her strengths and interests there, how she had met Jean-Yves.

She talked a lot about Jean-Yves. It was as if she needed to remember him right now, needed to call to mind how deep their love had been, how it had made her the woman she was. And to reinforce that, she talked about her children. She didn't know if he wanted to hear it or not. But she needed to say it.

"They're the most important things in the world to me now," she finished finally.

And Deke smiled at her over his wineglass, the fire reflected in his eyes, as he said, "I know what you mean."

And oddly she thought that he did. "Yes," she said, "you would, being a father yourself. I'm a little surprised," she admitted, "since you used to say you never wanted to be."

Deke rubbed the back of his neck. "You weren't half as surprised as I was."

Erin's brows lifted. "You mean you had to get married?"

"I never got married. Last summer a social worker showed up on my doorstep and told me I was a dad."

Erin stared at him. *"What?"*

Deke's mouth twisted. "Shock of my life." And then he told her about the woman called Violet who had been Zack's mother.

"She'd always said, No strings. She didn't want any herself. First thing she said to me when I met her in California was, 'I'd like to go to bed with you, but I don't want you getting ideas.'" He made a wry face, looking almost embarrassed to say the words. Was that a flush creeping up above his collar?

Erin was fascinated, and reluctantly impressed by Violet's no-nonsense approach to getting what she wanted. God knew Erin had always been totally unable to make moves like that herself.

"Outspoken, that was Violet," Deke said. "She was as free a spirit as I've ever known, always heading off into the sunset. The Lone Ranger had nothing on her." He studied the fire again, then lifted his glass and drained it. "But she always came back. Every couple of years she'd breeze through Santa Fe and we'd…spend a little time together."

Erin felt a stab of jealousy for this woman who had so easily breezed in and out of Deke's life. She didn't say anything. Just waited. And eventually Deke went on.

"I thought it was what I wanted, too. Consenting adults and all that. I don't expect you to understand. You were always the marriage and kids type. But I figured it would work for me. Violet said she couldn't have kids. Some doc had told her that when she was a teenager. She'd been a horsewoman in those days. Got thrown and stomped. Hurt bad. And a doc said kids weren't going to happen. Obviously he was wrong." Deke poured himself another glass of wine, then topped off Erin's.

"Maybe that was why she decided to see the world," he reflected. "Because she could—and no one would be coming along and slowing her down. But then someone did. Zack."

"And she didn't tell you?"

"Nope. Guess she figured I wouldn't want to know. She knew I wasn't interested in becoming a dad, although I remember once she said the same thing you used to say—" he looked at her then "—that I didn't have to be like my old man."

"And we were right."

"Thank God." He swallowed, stared into his glass, then at the fire.

Erin studied his profile, drank in the sight, wallowed in the moment. "Do you want to talk about it?"

His mouth twisted. "About what happened tonight, you mean? What about last night? Or the night before?"

She hadn't realized they'd all been bad. Impulsively Erin laid a hand on his arm. "Oh, Deke."

She ached for him, always had. Her own parents had been so unstintingly supportive of both her and her brother that she couldn't wholly fathom how awful it would be to have a father who belittled all your efforts to be the best person you could be.

She knew he didn't want her pity. He just wanted someone to talk to. So she was surprised when he laced his fingers through hers. His thumb rubbed absently against the back of her hand.

"I'm sorry," she told him. "I'm so sorry."

He shrugged. "Me, too. But I can't change anything. I thought I had that figured out after Thanksgiving when he cut me dead. And then, damn it, he showed up tonight! Why the hell did he do that?" He looked at her, anguished.

"Maybe he realized he'd hurt you."

Deke snorted. "Why would he care now?"

Why not the hundred other times? And Erin didn't know the answer to that. She squeezed his hand, wishing there was something else she could do.

Deke's jaw was clenched so tightly she saw the muscle pulse. Then he shook his head. "It doesn't matter. I just need to make sure I never do the same thing to Zack."

"You won't."

"I'll do my damnedest not to!" He shifted to face her, bringing one knee up onto the sofa between them. Their still-clasped hands rested on his thigh. "I'll try to do as good a job as you have."

Erin sighed. "I'm not always sure how good a job I'm doing."

"But they're great. And Gabriel likes *Raiders of the Lost Ark,* so you obviously did something right."

"He owes that to Jean-Yves. They always watched it together."

"I knew he was a good man."

Erin nodded. Now it was her turn to stare into the fire. "I wish he was here. It's so hard alone…."

"But you've got Taggart here and your folks."

"Yes. But they have their own lives. I don't want to impose."

"I doubt they think it's imposing. They love you."

Erin nodded. "I know that. But I'm the ultimate decision maker. It was my decision to move back here."

"A good one, obviously."

"I hope so. The kids wanted to come, too. They like playing cowboys." She shook her head, bemused, but her throat felt tight. "But sometimes I feel like I should have stayed. For Jean-Yves."

"Who wasn't there anymore," Deke reminded her.

"I know. But it's their heritage!"

"You can take them back for visits. They came here to visit, didn't they?"

"Yes. Every year." Erin sighed again. "It's just…"

But she couldn't explain. She'd felt adrift since Jean-Yves's death, as if her anchor was gone, as if she had no purpose anymore. It wasn't true, of course. She had the children to raise. She had her photography—if she ever got back to it. But it wasn't the same.

She and Jean-Yves had shared so much on so many levels. And now…now she just felt alone.

Deke's free hand—the one that wasn't holding

hers—came up and touched her hair. His fingers trailed down to her jaw, then lingered on her cheek. His touch was gentle, soothing. It offered solace, connection.

Common sense—self-preservation—told Erin she should pull away, that she should pour some more wine, let the dog out, let the cat in. Do anything other than sit there and let her feelings swamp her.

But she couldn't seem to move. She couldn't resist his touch. She had been so lonely. It had been so long. She had been nearly three years without any man's touch. And Deke's fingers on her cheek were something she had dreamed of. She turned her head. Her lips brushed against his palm.

He shifted his weight, moved his leg, and their clasped hands rested against the inseam of his jeans. Erin swallowed. She should turn away, pull back. She stayed. She shut her eyes.

"I wondered sometimes," Deke said, his voice low and a little husky. "I thought about you. Wondered where you were. What you were doing."

Missing you, she thought. *Wanting you.*

At least at first—before she'd managed to move on, to realize that there was more to life than unrequited love, that there were wonderful men in the world—at least *one* wonderful man in the world—besides Deke Malone.

"I thought about you, too," she said. If he only knew! Yet how generic she made it sound. How necessary it was to say it that way.

"Did you ever wonder…?" Deke stopped, letting his words trail off. His thumb brushed against her cheek; his fingers grazed her chin. He tipped her head so that she knew if she dared to open her eyes, she would be looking right into his.

She had to. Couldn't resist. And saw that his normally deep-blue eyes had darkened even more now. His gaze was intent.

She held herself steady under the light touch of his fingers, willed her heart to stay calm, her mind to be rational. "Wonder?" she echoed in barely more than a whisper. "Wonder what?"

Deke shook his head wordlessly. His thumb brushed her lips as slowly he moved closer. His face was mere inches from hers; his head blocked out the light from the fire.

But who needed light when she had a gaze full of Deke—of his dark brows, his midnight eyes, his sharp nose and firm lips? He was so close she could feel his breath on her lips. So near she could almost taste them.

And then she did. He kissed her.

It was the kiss that once she'd dreamed of. A gentle, slow tender kiss. Tentative at first. An asking. A tasting. An exploration.

As if he'd wondered…and asked…and liked what he found.

The kiss deepened, became firmer, more sure and more inquisitive at the same time.

And Erin responded. She was helpless *not* to respond. Her lips parted. She remembered reading once that a person could benefit not only from real weight lifting, but from just thinking about weight lifting. The brain, scientists said, responded not just to what it had done, but to what it merely thought about doing.

Apparently so did her mouth.

She'd always wondered what it would be like to

kiss Deke Malone. *Really* kiss him—and be kissed by him—not those quick little friendly pecks on the cheek that went with friendships like theirs. In fact, she had spent long pleasurable hours imagining how they would kiss. And it seemed that she had a good, accurate imagination.

But reality was even better.

She could have kept on kissing him forever, savoring the feel of his lips on hers, of their hands locked together, of his fingers cupping the nape of her neck, then softly stroking her hair. She felt almost bereft when he drew back far enough so that his eyes looked into hers. A smile played at the corners of his mouth.

"Well, now," he said, looking a little surprised and extremely pleased. "Who'd have guessed?"

Me, Erin thought. *I guessed. Years ago.* But she didn't say it.

"Curiosity satisfied?" Erin managed, trying to sound tart and a little jokey, unsure where things were going from here, unsure where she wanted them to go.

Slowly Deke shook his head. "Not even close."

The words barely left his mouth before he closed the distance between their lips again and continued his exploration.

There was nothing tentative about this kiss. It was warm and hungry, yet slow and leisurely at the same time. Like a five-course Parisian restaurant meal, Erin thought, where every flavor was to be considered, sampled, nibbled, savored.

And not only his mouth explored, his fingers did, as well. He let go of her hand and tangled both of his in her hair. Then, he stroked her back; he traced the line of her ear. He kissed the line of her jaw and the hollow of her throat, and then he returned to her lips again, parting them once more so that his tongue touched hers. It teased. It tempted.

And Erin's own curiosity, aroused beyond even her fevered dreams and wild imagination, met his, touch for touch, move for move.

She slid her hand over the soft flannel of his shirt and felt the heat that radiated from his back. She rubbed her fingers along the worn denim inseam against his thigh.

Deke swallowed a groan. His breathing quickened, and he pulled back again to meet her eyes once more.

"Erin?" His voice had a ragged edge to it. He was looking at her as if he'd never seen her before.

Probably this Erin he never had. Probably this Erin was shocking his socks off. She would actually like to shock his pants off. The thought, spontaneous and unexpected, made a tiny laugh burst inside her.

"What?" Deke said.

Erin shook her head. "Nothing." No matter how grown-up she was, there were some things she still couldn't say.

He looked perplexed, a little worried. "It was funny? My kissing you?"

She shook her head, smiling, giddy almost. Deke Malone had kissed her! "It was wonderful."

There were some perks to growing up, getting older, having had a life, she decided. She was less self-conscious now, more honest. Capable of admitting what she wouldn't have dared to admit fifteen years ago. All her inhibitions seemed to have fled.

She tilted her head and, feeling oddly daring—was it the wine? she wondered—smiled at him. "You're a very good kisser."

The frank comment raised his brows, and he gave her a speculative look. A small smile played at the corners of his mouth. "I'm not too bad at other things, either." There was gentle but clear innuendo in his words.

"Aren't you?" Erin's own words seemed almost to catch in her throat. She wasn't used to flirting—wasn't even sure she was flirting. Was she daring him? Was she daring herself? She felt a heady breathlessness that was foreign and tantalizing at the same time.

Deke's expression grew serious. He stroked her hair, her ear, her jaw, angling her head so that she looked straight at him. "Do you want to find out?"

Did she want to make love with him? Is *that* what he meant?

Erin's brain buzzed. Her mind whirled. Go to bed with Deke Malone? Here? Now? Tonight?

It was all her teenage fantasies coming true. Or was it? Might it not destroy everything they'd ever had between them? Might it not turn into a nightmare instead of a dream?

And if it did, then what? she asked herself caustically.

He wasn't offering her forever. He wasn't promising happily ever after. He was offering sex. He was offering intimacy. Connection. Not forever. Just for now.

But still, to have all those things even once with the man she had loved more than any man on earth...

She had only to say yes. But...

She was Erin.

Erin could always think of a thousand buts, could always find a hundred reasons to play things safe, to refuse to admit how very much she wanted to see Deke Malone naked, to have the freedom to run her hands over his body, to feel him become, however briefly, a part of her.

Not an hour ago, she'd admired his friend Violet who had always been up-front, who'd gone after what she'd wanted, who'd grabbed life with both hands, who had, Erin thought with amusement, probably grabbed Deke with both hands!

And Violet had had his son. She'd had intimate memories of Deke. How much richer her life, short though it was, must have been because she had dared.

If loving Jean-Yves had taught her anything it was that even a brief love was better than none at all.

Now Erin smiled at Deke. She touched his cheek. "I'd like to find out," she said.

Deke's hand stilled. He cupped her jaw and stared deep into her eyes. His own reflected his surprise at her response. He didn't speak.

"Unless you don't want to?" she added, because all of a sudden she felt panicky, as if she'd been too forward.

Deke shifted her hand on his thigh a little higher. "Does it feel like I don't want to?"

Heat coursed into her cheeks. "Oh!"

"Yeah. Oh." He looked at the sofa. "Here?"

Erin got to her feet and held out her hand to him. "Come upstairs."

Her bedroom was at the top of the stairs. Across from it was the room she had put all her books and photos and work-related stuff in, hoping someday she might call it an office and not a catch-all. Beyond them was the bathroom and Sophie's room. At the far end of the hall was the large room that Gabriel and Nicolas shared, and two other bedrooms that she thought she might turn into two bed-and-breakfast rooms, if she could figure out how to carve another bathroom into the floor plan.

She wasn't thinking about that tonight.

She was thinking about the man who followed her up the stairs, who stepped into her room and closed the door behind him with a quiet, deliberate click. The room was in shadows cast by the pinkish glow that came from a single streetlight and a snowy night. She didn't turn on the light. Didn't—couldn't—move at all.

Deke put gentle hands on her shoulders and turned her to face him, then slid his hands down her back and drew her close, bent his head, kissed her again, deeply, longingly.

And Erin, raising her arms to wrap them around him, thought, *Yes. Yes. Just like this.*

She backed up one step, two, three, and fell back onto the bed, bringing Deke with her. They rolled together, touching, stroking, kissing, caressing. His hands slipped up under her sweater, walking their way up her ribs, then cupping the fullness of her breasts. His head dropped to brush against them.

If she leaned forward she could bury her face in his soft hair. She breathed deeply, caught a hint of woodsy shampoo, of snow and leather and something uniquely inexpressibly Deke.

She'd forgotten it. And yet, the minute she drew a breath, everything—the memories, the conversations, the feelings, the yearnings—all the details came flooding back. It was as if a dam had broken, a door, long shut, had opened.

And if she'd had the slightest qualm about what she was doing, about the wisdom of making love with this man here tonight, it fled. It was something she'd wanted so long that even knowing their loving would go nowhere, she knew she wouldn't regret it.

When she shut the door later tonight, when he got back in his truck and, tomorrow, drove off to New Mexico, she would have the memory.

But for tonight, for these few hours, she would have Deke.

She tugged at his shirt, pulling it out of the waistband of his jeans, then slid her hands up underneath, relishing the hot smooth muscles of his back, letting her fingers walk up his spine, knead his shoulders, caress the short hair at the nape of his neck.

He lifted his face and she kissed the line of his jaw, rubbed her cheek against the faintest hint of stubble there. He must have shaved right before he'd come to the opening. He'd looked urbane and professional, very nice indeed, but she liked him better in jeans and boots. She thought she'd like him even better out of them! The thought made her swallow a giggle.

"Laughing at me again?" Deke said gruffly, kneeling up and tugging her sweater up and over her head in one quick movement. Then he was kissing her breasts, nuzzling between them and dropping tiny kisses down her belly to the button of her jeans.

"Not laughing at you," Erin gasped when he drew a line with the tip of his tongue from her bra down to her navel. "Want you," she added breathlessly.

"Feeling's mutual." He pulled back and started to unbutton his shirt, but she stopped him.

"Let me."

Deke's hands dropped to his sides, his fingers hung loosely as Erin undid the buttons one by one, parting his shirt and leaning forward to kiss his chest, to breathe in again the scent of him, to nuzzle his hair-roughened chest, to touch her lips to his flat nipples. She felt a tremor run through him. His fingers curled into fists.

Then she ran her hands down his chest to his belt and unfastened it, her fingers trembling slightly, fumbling as she did so. But Deke didn't do it for her. His jaw was clenched as he held perfectly still, not even breathing.

Then she undid the button on his jeans and drew down the zipper. Her fingers strayed over the soft cotton of his boxer shorts. Deke's breath hissed through his teeth as his hips moved forward, pressing the hot, hard length of him against her hands.

"My turn," he said raggedly, and he reached around behind her to unfasten her bra. She felt a tremor in his fingers as he did so, and she knew satisfaction at the notion that he was no more steady than she was. Her bra fell away, and his fingers came around to stroke her breasts. Then he bent his head and he kissed them and bore her down on the bed once more. He made quick work of the button and zipper on her jeans, then peeled them down her legs.

The cool night air teased her feverish body, and Erin scrabbled to tug his jeans down, as well. He pulled hers off. But his own tangled in his boots, and he muttered under his breath.

Quickly she rolled to a sitting position again. "Cowboys do it with their boots on?" she teased.

He managed a strained laugh and grimaced. "Rather not."

"Then allow me." She pushed him onto his back and reached down to tug off first one boot and then the other and, after them, his jeans. But then she stopped, unable to take the last step, to hook her fingers in the waistband of his shorts and pull them down. She simply sat, staring, appreciating the hard, muscular body—all angles, planes and shadows—that was Deke Malone.

He lay on his back, watching her just as intently, his eyes hooded, his breathing shallow, short and quick, until he could stand it no longer. And then he held out a hand to her. "Come here," he said softly. It was an invitation, a beseeching.

And Erin stretched out alongside him and put her hands on him, and he stroked her ribs and slipped his fingers inside her panties and drew them down, then pulled off his own shorts. And they were naked together—heated flesh to heated flesh, mouth to mouth, heart to heart.

She and Deke Malone.

His name reverberated through her mind. The boy's body she had dreamed of so long, harder now, tougher, filled out—a man's body—pressed hers into the bed. And she knew the joy of it. Relished it. *Wanted it.*

She eased her legs apart, opening for him, touching him at the same time, stroking him, making him tremble and suck in a harsh breath, even as his fingers sought her. Her breath came quick and ragged, too, as he found her ready for him. He stroked her, teased her. And Erin squirmed, trying to draw him down, to bring him in.

"Wait," he muttered desperately. "Slow down."

Yes, of course. Slow down. Take it easy. Savor. Relish. Memorize.

She knew that. Of course she did! But saying it and doing it were two different things. What her mind wanted, her body resisted. Her body was hungry, desperate, starving. It wanted Deke. It wanted him now.

And his body had a hunger of its own. He was biting his lip, tensing, fighting release.

"Deke," she whispered. "Come to me."

Love me. The words she could never say echoed in her head. She wouldn't spoil it by speaking them. She knew better.

This was Deke whom she had always loved, Deke who was her friend, who wanted her tonight, who needed something from her now, something that she could give—and would receive herself.

It was enough.

He came to her then, let her guide him down, arched his back and she felt him shudder with the sheer pleasure of sinking into her warmth.

"Yessss." The word hissed through his lips and then, trembling, he braced himself above her and dipped his head to kiss her. A deep hungry desperate kiss, not leisurely at all. And then, with exquisite slowness, he began to move. His body caressed hers, his sweat-slick skin slid over hers.

And Erin rose to meet him, to embrace him, to welcome him and now—just now! just this once—shuddering, shattering, she made him her own.

No regrets. She had no regrets.

She'd wondered if she might. The seconds after her climax splintered her, in the moments after Deke had surged into her one last time and then collapsed, shuddering against her, Erin wondered if doubt would now set in.

It did not.

And as she lay there, stroking Deke's hard muscled back, learning the ridges and dips of his spine, the smooth hollow at the small of his back, while still she held him inside her, she shut her eyes and knew a sense of fulfillment.

Another time in her life it surely would have been wrong. When they were teenagers, making love with Deke would have been a mistake. She would have wanted more, needed more, hoped for things that Deke couldn't give her.

She'd had those things from Jean-Yves. She'd had love, pure and full. She'd had a relationship of heart and soul and body and mind.

She didn't expect those things from Deke now. She had his friendship still. And now she had this memory.

This time it had been right.

No, she didn't regret it any more than she regretted loving Jean-Yves. It had hurt losing Jean-Yves. The pain of it had nearly killed her. But she never regretted loving a man whose job had put him in harm's way. She would never wish she hadn't in order to have saved herself the pain.

It was the same with Deke now.

He might stay a few more hours. He might kiss her again, hold her close, might even doze with her for a brief time. But then he would rise. He would dress. He would touch her hair and kiss her lips and smile at her.

And then, inevitably, he would get into his truck and go.

And she would hurt.

Erin had no illusions about it. Tomorrow she would feel hollow. She would ache with missing him and wish she had him still. But at least she would have the memory. She would have this night. She would have to remember that when she watched him go.

Some things were worth the cost.

Chapter 6

She didn't sleep a wink all night.

While Deke had been there, lying in her bed—in her arms—there was no way Erin could have slept. She'd simply lain there watching him, savoring his presence, storing up memories, relishing every moment.

And after he'd left, when he'd kissed her goodbye at the door with a tender smile and a whispered "Take care, Erin," she'd gone back upstairs and crawled back beneath the quilts to wrap her pillow in her arms and relive it all again.

Until daybreak she tasted his kisses over and over, crushed the pillow to her chest and remembered the hard warmth of his body covering hers. She rubbed her cheek where his rough stubble had grazed hers and tried to recapture the sensation. And finally she buried her face in his pillow, breathing in the scent of him and feeling her throat tighten and begin to ache.

She resisted it. Refused to give in. She wasn't going to hurt. She wasn't going to regret anything. It had been worth it, damn it!

But simply lying there thinking about it was too hard to do. She was restless, unfocused, tossing and turning. She needed to *do* something. So, throwing back the covers, Erin jumped out of bed—and felt twinges where she hadn't felt twinges in a very long time.

They made her smile. They focused the restlessness. They were her secret—her memory of last night. It was a memory she would hold dear forever.

But now, Erin knew, was not the time. Last night she had, she assured herself, exorcized her past. She had a memory of Deke to take with her always. But she couldn't dwell on it—not even to the extent that she had dwelt on her marriage to Jean-Yves.

She had to face the future. She had to get on with her life.

Brimming with energy, she took a quick shower and went downstairs. She let the dog out, then started the laundry. Then she swept the stairs. When the kids got up, she fed them oatmeal and fresh fruit and muffins— practicing for possible bed-and-breakfast guests, she told them when they blinked at the more-lavish-than-usual spread. Then Taggart came by to pick up Gabriel and offered to take the others, as well.

"They can play with Will and Abby or watch the bull and bronc riding," he said.

Nicolas was eager. Sophie was bouncing. "I can help Becky baby-sit."

"Okay?" Taggart asked his sister. "I'll bring 'em back this evening."

"Fine," Erin said. While they were gone she would get something done, too. She had procrastinated ever since they'd come from Paris. She hadn't picked up her camera once. Editors had called her and she'd declined jobs. She hadn't been ready.

Now she was. Ready for something. She had to do something—or she'd spend the day thinking about Deke.

That was the long and short of it right there. And she knew she couldn't think about Deke. It wasn't productive. It wasn't helpful. Someday she could take out the memory and savor it. But not today. Not for quite a while yet.

So she threw herself into work. She started with standard household chores. She vacuumed the whole house, then dusted everything that wasn't nailed down. She washed the kitchen and bathroom floors. She would have cleaned the drawers and cupboards, but since she'd only stocked them a month ago, they weren't much of a challenge yet.

But still filled with restless energy, she went upstairs and resolutely began stripping the wallpaper off the walls of one of the empty bedrooms. If she was really going to try doing bed-and-breakfast, the first task was getting the rooms redecorated. The second would be to find a plumber who could figure out how to put another bathroom on the second floor.

By lunchtime she had both bedrooms stripped of wallpaper and had scrubbed down the walls. Next she tackled her potential darkroom, putting up the bookshelves Taggart had brought over for her, then unpacking boxes and putting books on the shelves.

All that was left were the slides and prints. Boxes and boxes of them. Hers and Jean-Yves's. She knew she had to go through them, sort them out. But it would be too emotionally draining to do it now—and not nearly physical enough.

So instead she went downstairs and made turkey soup for dinner. It would have been therapeutic, she thought, if she could have chased the turkey around the yard first. Then she baked banana bread—wishing she could have climbed the banana tree—and whipped up three kinds of cookies.

Then, still energized, Erin began breaking down the boxes she'd emptied. Now that was satisfying work! Whacking away at big pieces of heavy-duty cardboard was the best thing she'd done all day. She was going at it with relish when the door separating the kitchen from The Spa opened, and Celie Tucker poked her head in.

"What on earth are you doing? It sounds like you're dismantling the kitchen!"

"I'm cleaning," Erin said, straightening up and stretching, feeling those twinges again. She bent and went at the cardboard with renewed vigor.

"There's cleaning," Celie said, "and there's *cleaning*. What you're doing sounds distinctly like a major overhaul. I didn't think I left the place that dirty."

Celie had moved back in here after she'd quit her job on the ship and returned to marry Jace.

"You didn't. It has nothing to do with you. It's me." She wasn't going to explain about Deke. If anyone had noticed his truck here, they would think what they wanted, but she wasn't going to add to the gossip. So she just said, "I woke up this morning and realized I've been drifting ever since I got back to Elmer. I decided it's time to start."

"So you're spring cleaning in, what? November?"

"Yes."

But it wasn't the house Erin was spring cleaning. It was her life.

"I'm getting ready for Christmas," she told Celie as she finished whacking apart the last box and laid the pieces in a stack to take outside. She stood up and took a deep breath. "And I'm getting on with my life."

Celie grinned broadly. "I understand completely." And there was such fervency in her voice that Erin blinked.

Then she remembered that Celie had kick-started her own life not that many months ago by bidding on Sloan Gallagher at Elmer's charity cowboy auction. She'd actually won him, too, though it was her sister Polly who had married Sloan a few months later.

His marrying her sister hadn't seemed to bother Celie at all, though, from what Erin had heard people in Elmer say. Sloan had been the catalyst that had made her move on—not the goal she'd moved toward.

It would be the same for Erin with Deke.

The bells on The Spa door jingled.

"Ah," Celie said. "That'll be Alice, here for her perm. Catch you later. Don't work too hard."

But Erin fully intended to. She had to.

By the time she was done, the house was sparkling, the extra bedrooms were cleaned and ready to paint or paper, the boxes of slides were stacked on her desk to go through when she could bring herself to sit still. Soup simmered on the stove, bread cooled on the counter.

And the kids would be thrilled that she'd made each of them their favorite cookies.

And because it was that time of year, she'd managed to locate the Christmas ornaments they'd brought from Paris among the various boxes they'd stored in the attic. She lugged the boxes downstairs and put them in the closet in the front hall where they would be handy when they brought in the tree.

She glanced at her watch. It was nearly six. The kids would be home soon. She went back to the kitchen and tossed a salad to go with the soup. Then she set the table and lit a candle to go in the center of it.

Stepping back, she surveyed her accomplishments. Yes, things looked better. Less haphazard, more under control, more settled, stable. As if she had finally begun to put down roots.

Yesterday the house had looked as if any strong wind might blow them away. Today it looked like a home. Maybe the kids wouldn't notice. Maybe they'd never noticed that it hadn't. But Erin had felt it.

She considered pouring herself a glass of the wine she and Deke had drunk last night, to toast the future. She was ready to face it now—whatever it might bring.

Outside she heard a truck pull up and she smiled and turned at the sound of footsteps on the porch. But instead of the door opening, there was a knock.

Puzzled, Erin went to answer it.

Deke stood there, white-faced, with Zack in his arms. "It's my dad. He had a heart attack last night."

"He isn't gonna die," Deke said fiercely.

He'd been saying it for hours, trying desperately to

believe it, trying to be strong, upbeat and positive for his mother, for Milly, for everyone else.

"He's *not* going to die," he'd said over and over, willing it to be true, for them and—he had to face it— for himself.

"Of course he isn't," Erin said promptly, wrapping her arms around both of them, hugging Deke tightly while Zack wriggled in their embrace.

"Down!" he insisted. "Ge' down!" and wriggled some more so that Deke let him slide to the floor and toddle happily away while his father, as always, drew strength from Erin and, for the first time today, felt the terrible tension ease.

He was running on adrenaline and caffeine, hadn't slept since he'd got up yesterday. The past twenty-four hours alone had become a roller coaster—from the high of the opening to the low of his father's walking out to the high of making love with Erin to the low of coming back to Milly's shortly after three in the morning, hoping to slip in without waking anyone and discovering the whole house ablaze with light and Milly scrambling around to get dressed and rush to the hospital because their father had had a heart attack.

Now Erin pulled off his jacket and pushed him into a chair. "Tell me," she commanded. "What happened? When? How bad is he?"

And Deke tried to explain it—as much as he knew.

He'd driven back to Milly's, still dazed by what had happened between him and Erin, regretting that he'd had to go, yet knowing there was nothing else to do.

And he'd seen all the lights and been sure Zack had awakened and started screaming because his dad wasn't there. Deke had jumped out of the truck and hurried up the steps, prepared to apologize.

But when he opened the door, Milly practically flew at him. "Thank God you're back! I didn't know where to reach you. Mom just called. Dad's in the hospital. He had a heart attack!"

Deke felt as if he'd been punched.

Their father had had a heart attack a few years ago. It had been serious, and Deke knew it had been touch-and-go for a while. Milly and Dori had wanted him to come home then, but he had declined, insisting—probably correctly—that the shock of seeing him would be enough to kill the old man. But he was here now, and even after last night, he knew he had to go.

"Which hospital?" he asked Milly.

"Livingston." She was still in her nightgown, looking for her shoes. C.J. was crying. Zack was looking bewildered. Cash was getting dressed.

"Don't. You stay here," Deke said to them. "I'll go."

Milly protested. "We can all go."

"They don't need all of us there." He managed a faint grin. "Hell, we'd give the whole staff heart attacks." He took hold of his sister's shoulders. "I'll call you. I'll go and see how he's doing, take care of Mom and I'll get back to you. If she wants you there now, I'll say so. But it won't do any good being there, dragging the kids. If you'll keep Zack…"

Milly hesitated, but C.J.'s crying apparently got to her and she was looking a little pale. Morning sickness kicking in early, he imagined. Finally she nodded. "You'll call?"

"I promise."

He found his mother pacing in the corridor outside the ICU.

She ran to Deke the minute she saw him. "He didn't come home!"

"What?"

She clutched at his arm. "He went back to the store when he left the gallery. Said he still had work to do. He didn't come home and I...I went to bed! I didn't know! When I woke up just before two, he w-wasn't there! I called the store and he didn't answer. I got in the car and went over there. He was l-lying on the f-floor!"

She sobbed then, and Deke wrapped her in his arms and held her tight and said what he hoped were the right things. "But you found him, Ma. You got to him in time. It's gonna be okay. He isn't going to die."

They paced the corridor together the rest of the night. Nurses and doctors went in and came out. "So far so good," one told them.

Finally, just before dawn the doctor stopped to talk. "He's holding his own," he told them, patting Deke's mother's hand.

"He's not—" but she couldn't even ask the question.

The doctor smiled his best professional, encouraging smile. "We'll know more when we can run some tests. The next twenty-four hours are critical."

"Can we see him?" Deke asked.

"Five minutes."

His mother might have known what to expect. She'd seen this before. Deke hadn't. It was a hell of a shock. His father lay, gray and lifeless looking, shrunken under the sheet. With his eyes closed and his mouth open, he looked a hundred years old. He looked dead.

Deke stopped abruptly, but his mother moved

forward resolutely, going to stand by the bed. She reached for her husband's hand and folded it in hers.

His eyelids flickered, then opened. His mouth moved, but Deke heard no words.

"I love you," Carol told him, through her tears. "We'll beat this," she promised. "We beat it before." She squeezed his hand. "See, John. Deke's here."

His father's gaze flickered toward the doorway and found him. Their gazes met—which was more than they'd done last night, Deke thought. He also thought, *Throw me out, I dare you.* But of course he didn't say it.

His father's gaze slid away, back toward his mother. "Store?"

Deke ground his teeth. Naturally. What else would he be thinking about?

Carol patted his hand. "Don't worry. Milly will open."

"No, she won't," Deke said flatly.

At his words, both his parents' gazes swiveled toward him, their expressions shocked.

"Milly's home puking her guts out," he went on. "She's morning sick, in case you didn't know. Besides that, she's got C.J. and the job at Poppy's and more than enough to worry about without the damn store."

"Oh, dear!" His mother looked shocked at the news, and then censorious for the way he'd broken it. "Well then, I can—"

"You can't, Mom," Deke said. "You don't know the first thing about it." She'd taken care of the house. His father's life had been the store. "Besides, you should be here where the doc can talk to you if he needs to."

"Dori…" his father said faintly.

"Probably just got home after having driven most of the night. She isn't turning around and coming back."

"Then I—"

"Oh, yeah, right," Deke said. "You're just going to get up out of your hospital bed and open the doors at eight o'clock." He met his father's glare with a defiant one of his own. "I'll open the store."

"You?" His father's voice might have been weak, but it dripped disbelief.

"I think I know how," he said with an edge to his voice.

"Well, of course, dear," his mother said nervously. "But...are you sure?"

"I'm sure."

"Thought you were leaving," his father said.

"I was. I'm not now."

"But you hated the store," his mother began.

"I hated being told it was going to be my life's work." Deke's eyes never left his father's. "No one had a right to make that decision for me. But I can work there for a while. Until you're ready to come back."

Tell me no now, he said silently, *and I'm gone and I'm never coming back.*

But his father didn't say no. He said, "Why?"

Their gazes locked, dueled. Deke jammed his hands into his pockets and glared. "Think about it," he said finally. "Maybe you'll figure it out."

He turned on his heel and walked out then. He went to the store and opened it, wondering what the hell task he'd set himself even as he was fiercely determined to do it. He expected to feel the same oppressive revulsion he'd felt all those years ago the minute he set foot inside it.

In fact, he didn't. The store seemed smaller. More

quaint. Less formidable. And he felt confident. Determined. And capable. Not powerless as he'd often felt all those years ago.

Which just went to show what growing up could do.

He prowled around, checking things out, discovering that little had changed. His dad being basically a traditionalist, there wasn't any newfangled, computer-driven cash register to figure out. No one scanned bar codes in Malone's Grocery.

He got cash from the bank, filled the meat counter from the cold storage, then swept the floor as his dad had always done every day before opening. Evelyn Richards, who had worked as the checker since Deke was a boy, arrived on time and was shocked to see him. He explained about his father. That shocked her, too.

"And you're going to run things?" she asked over and over.

"I'm going to run things, Evie."

It was two minutes to eight when he flipped the sign in the door to Open. Minutes later Old Lady Larrimer came in. "Why, Deke Malone? My heavenly days! Is that you?"

He grinned crookedly, "It's me, Mrs. Larrimer."

Deke coped all day. And when Milly finally dropped in with C.J. and Zack at five, he was still coping, cutting pork chops for a customer as if he'd done it every day of his life.

"I came to see if you'd survived," she said.

"I survived." Deke handed the man the package of chops.

She eyed him warily. "What about Monday? What about next week? Should we find someone?"

"We'll hire someone to help," Deke said. Because his

father would need that, regardless, when he recovered enough to go back to work. "But I'm staying."

He sat in Erin's kitchen an hour later and said it again. "I'm staying," he told her. "To help out. To run the store. I ran it today."

At least Erin didn't doubt. She didn't say, "You?" in an astonished tone of voice, even though she probably had more right to than anyone.

"Of course you're staying," she said. "Of course you'll help." As if it were a given. "And it will be easy. You'll be right there nearby, at your folks."

"Well, actually, that's the thing," he said awkwardly, rubbing a hand through his hair. He'd given it a lot of thought all the way up here. "I don't want to stay at my folks. While he's still in the hospital my mother will need to be there and I won't have any place for Zack. And when he comes home, I can't see it working—not me there with my dad, not to mention having a toddler around."

Erin nodded. "Yes," she said. "I see your point."

"I could stay at Milly's but the house is really small. We've been on the sofa, Zack and I, since we got there. And Milly's been so morning sick…"

"Right, I forgot about that. Poor Milly."

"Exactly." He waited, smiling optimistically, hoping the penny would drop. But Erin just stood there silent as a post, and finally he had to ask, "So what if we stayed with you?"

Chapter 7

No!

The word screamed inside Erin's head. In fact, she was so stunned by his request that her lips seemed welded shut.

The news of his father's heart attack had shocked her. Deke's decision to stay and run the store, while certainly admirable, brought her up short. She'd been convinced he was leaving today, that's why she'd dared make love with him last night. And now he was going to stick around?

And he wanted to stay with her?

Good God Almighty!

"I'll be happy to pay you for rooms," he said when she didn't speak.

As if that was the problem!

"I'm not—you don't—we're not a B and B!" she managed, stumbling over her words.

"I know that. But you've got extra rooms, and you said you were thinking about it the other night."

"I said that?" Well, yes, she probably had. "But it's not official! We don't even have an extra upstairs bathroom."

Deke shrugged. "I'm used to sharing."

There were other reasons—*lots* of reasons!—not to agree. But before she could articulate any of them, there was real pounding of feet on the steps outside this time. And the back door flew open and Gabriel, Sophie and Nicolas burst into the room.

"Zack!" Sophie was clearly thrilled, swooping down on the little boy who beamed just as happily at her. "What are you doing here? I thought you left."

"Change of plans. We're going to be here awhile," Deke answered for him. "My dad had a heart attack. He's in the hospital and I'm going to be running the grocery store."

Sophie looked dismayed. "I'm sorry about your dad. But I'm glad you're going to be here. Maybe I can babysit Zack sometime?"

Oh, don't. Don't do this, Erin pleaded silently with her daughter. But it was clearly too late.

"Maybe you can," Deke said. "I was talking to your mother about staying here."

Unfair, Deke. And from the speculative look on his face, Erin knew he knew it, too.

"Here?" Sophie's eyes were like saucers, and Erin could almost see the wheels spinning in her brain.

"And I was explaining how I'm really not prepared

for bed-and-breakfast guests at the moment," Erin said firmly

"But he wouldn't be a guest," Sophie protested. "He's a friend."

"We have *one* bathroom upstairs," Erin reminded her. "Who is it who's always yelling at her brothers to hurry up?"

"Well," Sophie said with a toss of her head, "they should. And when Deke and Zack stay, they'll have to. Besides, they could go downstairs and use the one down here."

"Or we could," Deke offered.

"Or you could," Erin said pointedly to her daughter.

"And I will if I have to while Deke and Zack are here." Sophie was all accommodation now. "So, great. It's settled!"

"I don't—" Erin began.

"Then we can watch the *Raiders* stunt video," Gabriel said suddenly, and he actually sounded eager to do so.

Nicolas's eyes lit up. "Do you like it, too?" he asked Deke just as eagerly.

"It's my favorite."

"Cool," Nicolas cheered. "So, he can stay then, right, Mama?"

Erin could feel the ground sliding away beneath her. She hadn't seen Gabriel look so eager for anything since the day Jean-Yves took him sailing. And Nicolas and Sophie were clearly for it. But they hadn't once been in love with him. He hadn't spent last night in their beds!

She made one last-ditch attempt. "The rooms aren't ready. I stripped the wallpaper off today. I scrubbed the walls. They're still wet. They smell like paste. The rooms are bare."

"We can move in furniture," Nicolas said.

"And fix up one room at a time," Gabriel added.

"We'll help," Sophie said. "I'll watch Zack after school so you can paint or paper."

They all looked at her avidly. Erin looked helplessly at Deke, hoping that he would say he didn't want to sleep in a room that smelled like paste.

He shrugged. "I don't mind roughing it. And Gabe's right. Zack and I can use one room while you work on the other. I'll help you work."

"I don't need your help!"

She could tell from his startled look that her vehemence was way out of line. "I meant," she said slowly, "that I can't possibly expect you to have time to help me with the rooms when you've got the store to deal with."

"But he can stay, can't he?" Sophie pressed the point.

"I don't mean to take advantage, Erin. I can get someone else to baby-sit Zack."

"Zack," Erin said recklessly, "is not the problem."

Deke raised his brows. All three of her kids looked far too interested in what exactly the problem was. Erin felt her face begin to burn.

"Never mind," she said. "It's just… Never mind." Bad enough she'd stuck her foot in her mouth. Did she have to shove her whole leg in there, too? "You can stay."

"Yippee!" A bilingual cheer went up from the kids. Even Zack realized something momentous had just happened and clapped his hands. Deke smiled, clearly pleased.

"There will be ground rules," Erin said, cutting off the celebration.

The kids looked at her. "What ground rules?"

Erin lifted her chin. "We will discuss it. Later. Right now you three need to get cleaned up. You're all filthy. Showers before dinner."

"But—" Gabriel looked hungrily at the bread on the counter.

Nicolas rubbed his belly. "I'm starving."

"Moi, aussi," Sophie agreed.

"If you're starving you'll just have to hurry before you perish then, won't you?" Erin said briskly. "Go on now. Scoot. Hurry. *Vite!*"

"Ground rules?" Deke said, watching her back as she stood, hands on hips, and listened to the pounding footsteps recede up the stairs.

She jumped at the sound of his voice. Her shoulders stiffened and she spun around. "Ground rules," she repeated, the color still high in her cheeks. "That's right."

Deke arched a brow. "What sort of ground rules? Take off my hat at meals? In before midnight? Wash the dishes I get dirty?" He paused. "Or do you mean you want ground rules because of what happened last night?"

He hoped she'd instantly deny it. But her expression immediately became shuttered. And for the first time Deke felt a twinge of regret.

As wonderful as their night together had been, if Erin was wishing it hadn't happened, then he did, too. The whole of their relationship meant more to him than it did. He didn't want to have blown their friendship over it.

"What about last night?" she said at last, and she didn't look destroyed, only dismissive. She shrugged. "It was a one-off, wasn't it?" Her gaze challenged him. "I mean you needed... And I wanted—"

She didn't finish the sentence, though Deke desperately wished she had. What had she wanted? A man's touch? *His* touch? As much as he would have liked to hear it, he didn't imagine he ever would.

He thought he knew exactly what she'd wanted last night—a man she liked in her bed because she couldn't have the one she loved. As much as he didn't want to think it, he knew he had been a replacement for her husband. She'd been lonely. And she was right—he'd needed her touch, as well.

"Listen," he said now, trying to pick his way through the emotional minefield and say the right thing to put her at ease. "It was great. But I didn't ask to stay because I expected—" No, he couldn't say it that baldly. He tried again, this time agreeing with her since that was what she seemed to want. He nodded his head. "Of course it was a one-off," he said in an attempt to reassure her. "Not that it wasn't..."

No, that wasn't any better. Hell!

This was what happened when you slept with a woman who was your best friend!

But then Erin surprised him. "Yes, it was great," she agreed just as firmly. "Very, um, nice indeed." She colored slightly. "But you were leaving, Deke. I never thought... I mean, even though you're staying, we can't...my kids...I won't...!"

"Of course not! I understand that."

"And I never meant…"

"I know," Deke cut in fervently. He didn't need her to spell it out.

They stared at each other. The color was high in Erin's cheeks now, and Deke could feel his own burn.

"Look," he said, trying to get it right this time. "We've been friends for a long time. I don't want to wreck that for anything. Not even last night. And I don't want to make things difficult for you. So if my staying here is going to make you uncomfortable, I won't do it. I'll stay at my folks'. Or when my dad comes home, I'll rent a room in Livingston or go back to Milly's."

"No."

He raised his brows at her uncompromising reply.

Erin shook her head firmly. "We are friends. You're right. I was being foolish." She smiled wryly and raked a hand through her hair. "Of course you're staying here."

He smiled, relieved. "And the ground rules?"

"Only one," she said, giving him a level look. "You stay in your bed and I'll stay in mine."

There. They had that settled.

Now, Erin assured herself after Deke left to go back to the hospital that evening, everything would be fine. But even as she told herself that, the future that she focused on this afternoon—the one she had been ignoring for so long—seemed remote and unreachable and on the far side of Deke.

And Deke, for his part, seemed like the embodiment of an alligator-infested swamp that she was going to have to cross to get there.

"Let it be a challenge to you," her dad always said when Taggart had come up against a bull he despaired of riding or when Erin had had to do a project for school that seemed impossible.

She had said it to herself innumerable times—when she'd been homesick upon first arriving in Paris, when Jean-Yves had departed after their marriage for his first assignment overseas, when he had died and she'd been faced with an uncertain future and three children to bring up alone.

She'd managed that. So far.

She could do this.

"We'll do fine, won't we?" she said to Zack, whom she'd been carrying around for the last half hour.

"Da?" Zack said worriedly. He should, by rights, have been asleep hours ago. He'd been fine while Gabriel and Sophie and Nicolas were up. He loved following them around, and they all, even Gabriel, enjoyed playing with him. But even though it was Saturday night and they had stayed up a little later than normal, their day helping out at the bull-and bronc-riding school for Uncle Taggart had worn her children out.

Nicolas fell asleep on the floor while the others were playing with the Western town. Gabriel and Sophie yawned repeatedly, and finally Erin chivvied them all off to bed. All but Zack who, now that the kids weren't there to entertain him, suddenly began to miss his father.

Erin had hoped he might go to sleep, too. But so far—and it was now nearly eleven—he was as wide awake as ever.

"Da?" he said again. "Dadddd?" His blue eyes grew wide and worried. His tone, at first hopeful, was getting sad and wistful.

"Shh, now, lovey. It's okay." Erin hugged him against

her chest and walked the room with him. He seemed to be running on the same adrenaline his father had been running on. And Erin suspected that any minute it was going to overcome him and he was going to dissolve into tears of frustration, anxiety and exhaustion. So she held him and cuddled him and tried her best to soothe him. She walked him and sang to him and told him about his father.

"Your da will be back soon," she promised him. "He's just gone to see Grandma and Grandpa. Do you remember Grandma and Grandpa?"

"Guh-ma?" Zack said tearfully.

"That's right. And Grandpa. Grandpa's in the hospital. Have you ever been in a hospital? Other than when you were born, I mean? I hope not. You don't want to learn about hospitals too early. Your dad knows about hospitals, though. I took him to one, once. Do you want me to tell you about it?"

Zack stopped fussing and started listening. So Erin proceeded to tell him all about one of the summers when Deke had worked at the ranch. He'd been riding a young horse to give it some exercise, she told Zack. It had been skittish all morning, but what finally spooked it was the sight of a plastic bag blowing in the wind.

One minute Deke had been in the saddle, and the next he'd been lying in the dirt. His arm had snapped, and he'd appeared to have an extra elbow. His face had been absolutely white.

"Stay there! Don't move!" she'd said, leaping out of the saddle to help him.

And he'd glared at her, furious and embarrassed. "Of course I'm going to move," he'd snarled. "I can't lay here all day." He'd got right up, taken one look at the bone poking through the flesh and fainted dead away.

"He was very brave, though," she told Zack. "When he finally did come around, even though it hurt terribly, he didn't cry at all. Just like you," she told him. "You've been stuck here with us all evening and you don't even know us, and you're being brave, too." She gave his nose a quick kiss.

Zack stuck his thumb in his mouth and leaned his head against her shoulder, and they continued to walk. She'd done this with Gabriel, with Sophie and with Nicolas. It felt oddly right to do it now, as if Zack, too, were her child.

Don't even think it, she warned herself. And she did her best to try not to. But all those long-ago dreams she'd tucked away in some dusty corner of her mind seemed to wriggle out now, to flicker to life again, to taunt and tempt her.

Zack's small body relaxed against her, going limp as exhaustion overcame him. He sucked sporadically on his thumb, but more often his jaw was slack, and every now and then a short sigh escaped him. Erin patted his back and cuddled him close, then slowly mounted the stairs to put him down in bed.

Bed was actually a mattress on the floor. She hadn't seen any need at all to bring the baby bed from Paris, so she hadn't had one to offer. Taggart had two, she'd told Deke over dinner. They could get one tomorrow.

But Deke had said it wasn't necessary. "No point. He'll climb right out. It's his latest trick, isn't it, buddy?" He'd tickled Zack's ribs, and the little boy had giggled gleefully.

So instead Erin had put a mattress on the floor across

the room from the bed she'd made up for Deke. Then she'd put a sheet on the mattress and had placed a rug next to it so Zack wouldn't hit the hardwood floor with a thump if he rolled off.

"Not a matter of if—but when," Deke had said approvingly when she'd shown him. Erin, remembering her own kids' nocturnal migrations at that age, supposed he was right.

Now she knelt and settled Zack on the mattress. He whimpered, shifted around and flung out an arm, but he didn't wake up. Still Erin stayed beside him, ready to soothe him if necessary until she was sure he was fast asleep.

She stroked a hand over his silky hair and touched the satiny skin of his cheek. Such a beautiful child. "Good night, sweetheart," she whispered and kissed him.

Who'd have thought, twenty-four hours ago, that she'd be kissing Deke Malone's child good-night?

Deke got back at quarter past midnight. The porch light was on and there was a light in the entry hall. He presumed that meant "come in the front door." So he did.

The house was silent. No Zack crying, thank God. He eased the door shut quietly, then tugged off his boots and stuck them under the bench with the rest. Then he shed his hat and jacket, shut off the light and padded softly up the steps.

Outside Erin's door, he stopped, tempted mightily, remembering last night. Remembering Erin. Wanting her.

Last night she had wanted him.

No, he reminded himself. She hadn't. Not really. She liked him. He was a friend. And maybe just that once— last night-a lover.

But not the man she loved. Not the man she missed.

He could make her forget, Deke's tempted self argued. He could make her happy, however briefly.

But common sense and sanity told him that afterward both of them would be worse off than before. Erin had made her "ground rule" for a reason—because she didn't want them to take things in a direction they shouldn't go. Their night together had been a one-off—a night he was sure he would remember for the rest of his life—but a one-off just the same. Because it wasn't right for her.

So he stood there for one more moment, remembering— wishing—and entertaining the faintest hope that she might have heard him come up the stairs, that she might have changed her mind, that she might open the door or call his name.

But the door stayed closed and the night stayed silent.

And finally Deke dragged himself down the hall and into the room he was sharing with Zack. His son lay fast asleep half on, half off his mattress. Slowly and carefully, so as not to wake him, Deke maneuvered him back onto it. He brushed a hand across the boy's hair, then stood up again and stripped down to his shorts and T-shirt, then slid between the clean, cold sheets.

Last night at this time he had been in bed with Erin. What a difference a day made. He felt weary, exhausted and emotionally spent on account of his father. He ached, feeling deprived and bereft of the company of Erin. He also felt virtuous, honorable and noble.

He just wished virtue, honor and nobility were warmer companions.

"So Deke Malone is staying with you?" Felicity raised her brows when Erin carried Zack into her sister-in-law's kitchen the following morning.

It was Sunday and the grocery store wasn't open, but Deke had gone down to Livingston to the hospital. He'd been less than thrilled at the prospect, but when Erin agreed that it would be good to check on things, he'd gone and she'd kept Zack.

She'd brought him and the other kids over to the ranch after breakfast so hers could watch the last-day competition at the bull-and bronc-riding school and so she could pick up a high chair for Zack.

"Yes," she said, "just for a few days."

"Nice that you had room for them," Felicity said. "It's a little cramped at Milly and Cash's, and I don't suppose Deke wanted to stay at his folks'. Taggart was amazed to hear Deke was running the store at all. Said he'd always hated it."

"Yes, well, you know how it is…when the chips are down…"

Felicity nodded. "Will called him 'a good man to ride the river with.'"

"Dad always did like Deke."

"He seems really nice. Not to mention one of the best-looking men I've ever seen. I had no idea."

Erin, who certainly agreed, wasn't quite sure what to say to that, so she just settled Zack among Willy's trucks and tractors and toy cowboys and horses.

"Coffee?" Felicity offered, and at Erin's nod she went on. "How long is he staying?"

"Not sure. We don't know how long his dad will be laid up. Of course he'll be back to work as soon as he can. They'd have to nail him in a coffin to keep John Malone out of that store for long. And I know Deke won't work there when he gets back. Evelyn Richards works half days apparently, but Deke said he's going to have to find someone to work full-time." She took the mug Felicity handed her and sat down at the table and took a sip. "That's what he's talking to his dad about today. So I suppose when he gets the right person and trains them, and his dad is out of the woods, he'll go. A week…maybe two."

She was dealing with this, day by day, so she didn't have a good answer.

"Maybe he'll stay for good," Felicity murmured. "If you and he…" She let her voice trail off, but her smile was speculative.

"If he and I…?" But then the import of Felicity's smile hit her, and the coffee in Erin's mug sloshed all over her hand. "What!" she exclaimed. Then, "Ow!"

Felicity tossed her a dish towel to mop up with and pressed on. "It only makes sense. I mean, you're unattached. He's unattached. You're beautiful. He's drop-dead gorgeous. You have careers in common. Kids in common. Need I go on?"

"No!"

They were good in bed together, too. But she certainly wasn't telling Felicity that! "It doesn't mean anything," she said firmly. "Two people don't get 'serious' because they have things in common, for heaven's sake!" But Erin could feel her cheeks burn even as she spoke.

"Really?" Felicity gave her a bemused look.

"Really!"

"You don't think you're perhaps protesting a bit too much?"

Well, yes, but... "I'm protesting because it's true!" Erin said fiercely. "Besides, I need to nip such unwarranted speculation in the bud. I don't want anyone getting ideas!"

"Right." *Not,* she heard in Felicity's voice.

"Deke and I are friends. We've *always* been friends. Taggart must had told you that," Erin said a little desperately.

"Yes." Felicity nodded as she regarded Erin gravely over the top of her own coffee mug. "He also said you were well suited."

"Taggart said that?" Since when had Taggart even thought about her eligibility and who would make a good husband for her. "This is my brother we're talking about. Can you spell clueless? *T.A.G.G.A.R.T.* Trust me, affairs of the heart have never been Taggart's forte."

Felicity laughed at that, but then she sighed and got a little dreamy-eyed as she said, "He has his moments."

"I'm glad to hear it," Erin countered dryly. But she didn't want to think about her brother's love life any more than her own.

Felicity laughed again. "Don't worry. I won't bore you with it. But it's true. So—" she changed tack "—you and Deke are happy just being friends?"

"Of course." But as she said the words, she looked away. Checking on Zack, she told herself, needing to see what he was up to. Mostly, though, needing *not* to look Felicity straight in the eye right then.

"You don't want more?" Felicity pressed. "You don't want another relationship ever?"

"I told you—and Mom—that I'm not looking for another man. I had the best man imaginable."

"So did I," Felicity said quietly. Her own first husband, Dirk, she meant. Now she stared out the kitchen window across the yard to where she could see her current husband moving bulls into the indoor arena. "And now," she said with a gentle smile, "I have another one."

"Taggart?" Erin scoffed at the thought of her big brother being anyone's idea of "the best man imaginable," even though she had to admit that Felicity and Taggart were perfect for each other.

"Taggart," Felicity affirmed staunchly. "Truly," she added, when Erin continued to look skeptical. "Even though I'll be the first to admit that he is not the sort of man I expected to marry at all."

"Well, Deke was *exactly* the man I expected to marry fifteen years ago," Erin said recklessly, determined to prove to Felicity that she and Deke were nothing like Felicity and Taggart.

"So, you were in love with him."

It wasn't a question. There was an "I thought so" tone in Felicity's voice. She eyed Erin narrowly, and Erin wondered if her candor had been a mistake.

"I was infatuated with him," she corrected. "And, like you said, he was gorgeous. He was nice and friendly and talented and we spent a lot of time together. He used to talk to me about cowboying and photography and his father. He used to talk to me about his girlfriends," she added wryly.

"Ouch."

"Well, yes. At the time it felt very much like ouch. But—" Erin tried to sound airily indifferent now "—I survived. I got over it. I got over *him*. I went to Paris and met Jean-Yves. And the rest is history. That's when I really fell in love."

Which was true. It had taken a year or so in Paris for her to put Deke totally behind her, but she had done it. And she hadn't regretted it. When she and Jean-Yves had begun to get serious, she was ready for it. She hadn't looked back.

"And now?" Felicity prompted.

"And now nothing. He's staying with us for a few days. That's all. Look," she said before Felicity began to argue or start a campaign to get her and Deke together, "you're right. I was attracted. I was infatuated. But Deke was *never* infatuated with me."

"Back then," Felicity agreed then added, "He might have changed."

Erin shook her head. "No."

She wished she could say that nothing had changed. But it had—they'd made love.

But even though he'd gone to bed with her, even though they'd made love, even though Erin found she still had feelings for him and would have given a great deal to think that her feelings were reciprocated, she didn't believe it.

Deke wasn't the falling-in-love type. He'd had girlfriends—lots of girlfriends—but he'd never been in love with any of them. He hadn't even loved Violet,

Zack's mother. He admitted it. They'd been "good friends." Nothing more.

That was all Deke wanted. All he'd ever wanted—from Violet, from all the girls he'd known long ago, from all the women he'd known since. *And* from her.

"Men change," Felicity insisted. "They grow up."

"Some do," Erin allowed. She took a swallow of her coffee. "But not this man. Deke doesn't want to get married. He never did. He never wanted kids."

"Well, see? That proves what I said," Felicity argued. "He has changed. He's clearly besotted with Zack."

"It's not the same."

"I don't see—"

She wasn't explaining about Deke and Violet. That was something private Deke had shared with her. But it meant that she was right about his intentions.

"Deke never wanted family," she said firmly. "Too many demands. Too much pressure. Taggart told you about his dad…" She shook her head. "He didn't want to have any part of that."

"Then why…?" Felicity began, then glanced over at Zack, and a glimmer of understanding began to light her eyes. "Oh."

"So don't get your hopes up. And I'm not getting mine up. It wouldn't make sense."

Felicity looked as if she were going to argue more, but eventually she just sighed and made a wry face. "Maybe you're right," she conceded. "Maybe I'm just too much of a Pollyanna these days."

"Yes," Erin said. "You are."

But Felicity's admission wasn't as comforting as Erin would have wished.

She stood abruptly. "I need to go home and get to work. Come on, Zack. Let's get going."

Zack, who had been making brrrmm-brrrmm noises with one of Willy's trucks, looked up. "Play truck?" he said hopefully.

"We'll come visit another day, and maybe Willy will be able to play with you then. We have to go now."

"Willy play? Go bye-bye?" His lower lip jutted. Blue eyes filled with tears.

"Oh, no, you don't." Erin scooped him up into her arms before he could begin to wail. "Yep, bye-bye. If we go now we have time to see the horseys first." She turned to Felicity. "If you'll carry him, I'll bring the high chair."

"I'll bring the high chair," Felicity said seeing Zack cling. "I think he'd rather stay with you."

They went to look at the horses. Erin told her kids to behave, then she joined Felicity, who was storing the high chair in the back of the Suburban. Deke had put the car seat in for her earlier. Now she settled Zack into it and expertly buckled him in.

"You're very good at that," Felicity said with a grin as Erin stepped back and shut the door.

"I've had a lot of practice. It comes back."

Felicity nodded. "I hope so." She said it so casually, so offhandedly that it took a few seconds for her meaning to sink in.

When it did, Erin turned to stare wide-eyed at her sister-in-law, who looked guilelessly back at her. Only the sparkle in her eyes gave her away.

Erin gave a shout. "Are you—" She gaped, astonished at the implication of Felicity's words. "You are!"

Felicity's mouth twitched into a tiny grin that quickly

widened until she seemed to be smiling all over her face. "Actually," she said, "yes. I am."

"*Mon dieu!* But, that's wonderful! Are you thrilled? When did you find out? When's the baby due? Is it twins?" The questions kept bubbling out.

"Yes, we're thrilled. A little surprised," Felicity admitted. "I thought it was possible, but I didn't want to think about it at all, what with getting ready for Thanksgiving and everything. So I didn't do a test until yesterday. I think the baby will be due in July sometime. And heaven help us if it's twins! I think Taggart will drown himself."

But for all that she winced as she said it, Felicity was clearly delighted. And Erin was delighted for her—for all their family. She even felt a tiny prick of envy at her sister-in-law's news.

It wasn't that she wanted another child. It was that she remembered the joy of anticipation, the sense of hope and unity that she and Jean-Yves had shared whenever they'd looked forward to welcoming a new child into their family.

She missed that unity, that hope, that anticipation. She missed having someone to share it with. *Jean-Yves*. She missed Jean-Yves.

So why for an instant did Deke Malone's hard features flash through her mind? She gave her head a quick, fierce shake.

She yanked open the front door to the Suburban. "We'll be sure to keep the high chair in good shape for the new arrival," she promised.

"Don't worry. We have two."

"We should have it back before Christmas," Erin

went on resolutely. She got into the driver's seat. "I'm sure Deke and Zack will be gone by then."

Felicity smiled at her. "Maybe not. Maybe Deke and Zack will like it here so much they'll hang around forever."

"You really are a Pollyanna," Erin said sternly.

Felicity looked positively beatific in her state of prenatal bliss. "Who knows? Christmas is coming, after all," she said, smiling. "It's the season of miracles."

Chapter 8

The best defense was a good offense.

Even if the man you were trying to mow down was flat on his back in a hospital bed, hooked up to machines and drugged to boot, if that man was John Malone, you had to come out with all guns blazing.

Deke knew he wouldn't get anywhere dealing with his father by tiptoeing around asking the old man his preference or soliciting his opinion. Doing that was a recipe for disaster.

So, as long as Deke was in charge of the store, things were going to be run his way.

And that meant hiring full-time help.

"I wrote an ad for the paper yesterday." He strode into his father's room already talking. "I'm hiring a butcher and a full-time clerk/stocker. Evelyn's fine, but she can't do everything. And she doesn't want to, in any case."

Evelyn, his father's only employee, was old enough to be Deke's grandmother. She worked part-time three days a week and she was reliable and conscientious, but she couldn't stock shelves because she had arthritic knees and she wouldn't work behind the meat counter because in her eyes that was "man's work."

"The ad will run starting tomorrow," Deke went on. "Hopefully we'll have enough applicants that I can weed them out on the phone and interview the best in the store sometime next week."

He paused then because he needed to take a breath. And he was fully prepared for his father to throw a fit, to toss out disparaging remarks, to behave in time-honored sarcastic John Malone fashion. *Hire help? After a day's work? What's the matter? Can't you cope?* That seemed the most likely jab. Or, *Too lazy to work all day yourself?* Another possible zinger. Deke was sure his father could think of others that wouldn't occur to him in a million years. He steeled himself, ready.

But his father didn't say a word.

Deke scowled, then jerked off his hat and moved closer to the old man's bed. "Are you all right?"

"Do I look all right?"

"You look like hell."

"Feel like it, too."

"Is that why you're not arguing?"

There was a second's hesitation, then John said, "I'm not arguing because you're right."

Deke stared. *I'm right?*

"I'm a realist, damn it." His father waved a feeble

hand. "Always have been. Look at me. I'm not going to be back twelve hours a day by the middle of next week."

"No, you're not." But Deke was still surprised, that his father would admit it. He cleared his throat, curious and a little worried. "So when can you come back? Did the doc say?"

"Don't know yet. He's doing the surgery on Wednesday. Guess we'll see how successful that is."

He said it offhand, but the great unknown of heart surgery had to be just a little terrifying. Certainly Deke felt his own brand of terror at the thought. As hard as his father was to deal with, at least he was there to be dealt with. He wasn't in a box and six feet under.

But expressing the slightest concern wasn't going to make the old man any happier. So Deke said, "I'm sure it will be fine. You'll probably be back in the store before Christmas."

"You hope," his father said.

They glared at each other, but the old animosity wasn't there. Deke almost thought he heard a grudging respect in his father's tone. But it was more likely, he reminded himself, in his imagination. He found it amazing that he was having any sort of conversation with his father at all.

He'd come from Elmer this morning at Erin's urging. "Go see your father," she had encouraged him. "Take advantage of having the upper hand for once."

Deke hadn't been sure how long his "upper hand" would last, but it had sounded like good advice, so he'd taken it. Not only because she was probably right about dealing with his father, but because all morning long she'd been like a cat in a roomful of rocking chairs where he was concerned.

When he'd walked into the kitchen with Zack, she'd been at the stove, stirring oatmeal. He'd been tempted, actually, to go up behind her and lift her hair and kiss the nape of her neck. Good thing he hadn't, because when he merely said, "Good morning," from across the room she'd jumped a foot.

Then she'd dashed off to exchange her bathrobe for jeans, and a long-sleeved shirt and a sweater, and her loose-flowing hair for a no-nonsense braid down her back. She looked like an old-fashioned schoolmarm, all starch and as sharp as new pencils. She handed him his coffee mug without touching him and had volunteered to feed Zack, carefully keeping herself on the far side of the high chair at every moment. As if it were a shield.

As if Deke were going to jump her bones at any moment.

Not that the thought didn't cross his mind. He was beginning to wonder where the heck his mind had been all those years ago that he hadn't spent hours lusting after her. Maybe it was because he'd been young and foolish and blindsided by more blatant females in those days. Whatever, Erin's charms were certainly apparent now.

And clearly off-limits as well.

He wasn't used to making her nervous. Didn't want to. But couldn't really confront her about it, either, not with the kids bounding down the stairs. So he'd taken her advice and left. Now he glanced at his watch again, wondering if he could go back yet.

"Where's Zack?" his father asked suddenly. It was the first actual acknowledgment of Zack's existence that the old man had made.

"With Erin Jones. She took him to her brother's today."

"Nice of her."

"She's a nice person," Deke said, daring his father to contradict him. He remembered all too well when his father had blamed Erin for "leading him astray" by getting the fellowship to Paris and "putting ideas in his head."

But the old man didn't argue with that, either. He just grunted. "You could bring him sometime."

Deke blinked. "Bring him? Zack? Here?"

"Milly brought C.J."

Several pithy things sprung to Deke's lips—all of which were sarcastic, learned from the master who lay looking at him now. He managed to swallow them all. "I could do that," he said. "If you want."

"Wouldn't mind."

Right. He couldn't possibly admit he wanted to see his grandson, could he? Of course not. "Okay," Deke said. "Speaking of which, I better get moving. Don't want to stick Erin with him all day."

"Could bring her sometime, too," his father said.

Deke felt his eyebrows twitch. Bring Zack? Bring Erin? Not argue? What the hell was going on? "Er, yeah. I'll mention it to her."

His father nodded. "G'wan now." He made a vague shooing motion with his hand. "Tirin' me out."

"Right. I'm gone." Deke headed for the door.

"Deke."

Deke glanced back.

His father was pointing a finger at him. "I don't want any slackers workin' in my store," he said. "Whoever you get, they'd better be willing to put in a hard day's work."

"For a good day's wages," Deke agreed. "They will."

"You check references. And work records."

"Uh-huh."

"No lowlifes."

"I won't take anyone with more than half a dozen embezzlement convictions," Deke promised.

His father opened his mouth, then snapped it shut again. He glared at Deke, but there was a telltale twitch at the corner of his mouth. "Scram."

Grinning, Deke did.

"Do you think he's mellowing?"

Deke tipped back his chair in Erin's kitchen that night after the kids had gone to bed, and relished his first chance to talk to her unchaperoned all day—unless you counted the angel costume, a former bed sheet that was presently being stitched and which seemed to be occupying most of her attention.

She gave him a quick glance, then began maneuvering the material through the sewing machine as she reflected on his brief rundown of the encounter with his father this morning. "Could be," she said. "Sounds like. Let's hope."

Deke rocked on the chair and watched her work. As he did so, he played idly with the camera he had brought down earlier to show Gabe. To Erin's obvious consternation, the boy had brought down his father's first camera after dinner and they had compared.

It had been a tricky moment. Deke had been interested in seeing Jean-Yves LaChance's first camera. He was curious about the man who had been Erin's husband. And he enjoyed talking to the serious, intense boy who was clearly interested in photography. In many respects he reminded Deke a lot of Erin.

But he could tell Erin wasn't happy with Gabe's having done so. She'd opened her mouth several times, as if she might want to cut off their conversation.

Because it hurt her to see him handling her husband's camera? Because it hurt her to remember the man she loved? To hear Gabriel talk about him eagerly and wistfully?

Yes, Deke could believe all of the above.

And he didn't want to hurt her. So he'd got out his own camera and had gradually led the discussion around to taking pictures. He'd offered Gabe his camera to shoot. The boy had been flatteringly eager.

And Erin had gone back to her sewing, able to ignore them now that Jean-Yves was no longer the topic of conversation.

Now Deke idly lifted his camera and aimed it at Erin, studying her through the lens. It always helped him to get a handle on things if he focused on them this way.

What he saw when he looked at Erin was a serious, intent, beautiful woman. She was wearing glasses, which added to that impression. He'd never seen her in glasses before. They made her look younger—and they made his fingers itch to remove them, to turn her face to look at him, to muss her long, dark hair.

He clicked the shutter.

She was sewing a seam, pressing the foot pedal and didn't notice. The sewing machine whirred madly as she guided the material and stitched the seam. He clicked the shutter again. And again.

Finally she finished the seam and glanced his way.

"What are you doing?" she demanded, noticing his finger on the shutter for the first time.

He shrugged. "Recording you for posterity."

Her cheeks turned pink. "Don't be ridiculous!"

"Not ridiculous. Makes perfect sense. Sophie said they were putting together a memory book of Elmer pageants. She even suggested I take pictures, if you recall."

"Of the pageant."

"And everything leading up to it," Deke said, snapping another of her, open-mouthed and red-faced. He grinned.

Erin glowered, then rolled her eyes and looked away again, focusing once more on the angel costume.

When she finally finished it, Deke said, "How about a glass of wine?"

"Can't," Erin said briskly. "Got work to do."

"All of it tonight?"

"Well, I don't get a lot of this sort of thing done during the day."

Because of Zack, obviously. "I know. I'm sorry. I—"

"I'm glad to have him," she said fiercely. "I'm just explaining. I told Mary Holt I'd have these done by early next week."

"Right," Deke said. He sighed. "Don't let me stop you."

She gave him an odd look. But then she went back to something she called a "cutting board," which she'd laid on the floor, and began to crawl around on it as she spread out another old sheet and started pinning a dismantled angel costume to it as a pattern. He could see it was going to be an all-evening project.

Well, fine. He'd work on his project, too. He got up

and wandered around the room, turning to snap another picture or two now and then. Every time he pressed the shutter, Erin flinched.

Finally she scowled over her shoulder at him. "Don't feel you have to stick around," she said through the pins she held between her teeth, "just because Zack is here. You can go out, you know. Go visit your sister. Go have a beer."

He shook his head. "No, thanks." He was getting into this. The view was much more interesting right here.

He wondered if Erin had any idea how enticing she was, crawling around the floor in her formfitting jeans with her bottom up in the air. Every once in a while when she stretched, her sweatshirt hiked up above her waist, and he got a glimpse of a thin band of the creamy skin of her back.

Deke was a visual sort of guy. His eye was trained to see and interpret, to seek out hints and ask questions. And that single narrow strip of flesh tantalized him. Every time it came into view, his gaze was riveted on it. It had all the allure of a glimpse of Victorian ankle. When it was all a guy saw, and it hinted at more, it drew his eye, tempted him, tantalized him.

Surreptitiously Deke eased the fit of his jeans. He tried to think of something else without actually averting his gaze, determined to enjoy the view without losing his cool—or his mind. If he wasn't going to get to have her undivided attention, she was certainly going to get his.

He watched. He snapped pictures. Finally Erin finished pinning the damn thing and began to cut. And as she moved, her bottom swayed. It bobbed up and down. The sight made his mouth dry and his palms damp and his jeans way too tight. So did the occasional glimpses of flesh at her waist.

He remembered the night he had seen more flesh. He remembered Erin naked. Remembered her lush curves and her long limbs wrapped around him.

Now she stretched and pinned and wiggled forward to pin some more.

Cripes, a man could only take so much. When had Erin Jones become a sex object? Deke slapped his camera down on the table. "I need to go for a walk!"

Detachment—that was the key.

Unfailing politeness, common courtesy, and determined detachment. If anything would get her through Deke's tenure in her house unscathed, Erin knew that was going to be it. And keeping a high chair or an angel costume or a coffeepot or a child between them at all times wouldn't hurt, either.

Because the trouble was that just having him in the house felt absolutely right. It was like playing house with the man of her teenage dreams.

He and Zack fit right in. They immediately "belonged" as if they had always been an integral part of the family. Deke handled her kids with ease. He talked photography and *Raiders of the Lost Ark* with Gabriel, he built a snowman with Sophie and Nicolas. And he treated her with his perennial casual charm.

And his son might as well have been one of her own. Zack followed her everywhere like a duck. He listened to everything she told him, absorbing her words like a sponge. He brought her books to read and tried to repeat the rhymes she told him. Every morning they fed the dog together and every morning they went out and fed and patted the bunnies in the hutch. They read again before his afternoon nap, and when he got up to find that Sophie and Nicolas and Gabriel were home from school and would play with him, he was in seventh heaven.

"We should keep him, Mama," Sophie said.

And though she knew they couldn't, Erin couldn't help feeling her daughter was right.

Every night when she kissed him good-night, Erin had to keep reminding herself that he wasn't her son, that he and his father *weren't* part of her family, that this situation was just temporary—and that no matter how right it felt, it was going to end.

Deke didn't make it easy for her.

He was gone a lot of the day, of course. But she saw him in the morning coming shirtless out of the bathroom. She saw him in the evening talking cameras with her son. She saw him build that snowman with Sophie and Nicolas and Zack. She saw him spend hours and hours after working in the store, talking with Milly about potential employees and trying to do things right for his dad.

One of the things she had always admired about Deke was his determined devotion to his dad.

It had always been easy to love her own father. Will Jones was an amiable, cheerful, happy man. He loved his family and made it clear in word and deed. And he inspired similar feelings in both Taggart and herself.

She thought it must be one of the hardest things on earth to persevere in caring about a man who seemed not to care about you.

"That's just the way he is," Deke said. Then he admitted, "Yeah, sometimes it hurts. Sometimes it hurts a lot. And I was ready to leave and not come back, but he did come to my opening…" He shrugged.

The words were unspoken: *So he must really care.*

Erin desperately hoped it was true. But even if it wasn't, believing it had made Deke a better man.

Besides if there was any doubt that his father cared about him, there was certainly no doubt that Deke cared about his old man. He, who had hated that store, was working ten-hour days dealing with the butcher shop and the groceries and interviewing potential employees. Then he came home and asked about her day with Zack, and about her kids as well.

She wished he wouldn't get involved with them. It would just make it harder when he left. But she couldn't say that.

And she couldn't regret the attention he paid them, either. He brought out things in them that neither she nor her brother or parents had tapped.

Gabriel, for example, who had never once talked to her about being interested in photography, talked to Deke about it nonstop.

But last Sunday when she and Deke had begun talking about photography before dinner—a determined effort on her part to keep things on a "friendly but detached" level with Deke—Gabriel came and listened. And the next thing she knew he disappeared upstairs, only to reappear moments later with a camera in his hands, saying to Deke, "Do you want to see my papa's camera?"

Erin had been astonished—and dismayed. So much for keeping things impersonal.

Especially when Deke had said, "Yes, I'd like to very

much," with exactly the right amount of respect and interest.

He had taken the camera from Gabriel, handling it almost reverently, telling the boy what a fine camera it was, how much better it was than the first one he'd had, and how he was sure Gabriel's father must have valued it highly.

"I guess he did. He said he always knew he wanted to take pictures," Gabriel replied.

And Deke nodded gravely. "It's a camera for a man who means business."

Gabriel hesitated, swallowed, then ventured, "Will you teach me how to use it?"

Erin very nearly blurted, *Why are you asking him? I can teach you!*

She had managed to keep her mouth shut—barely—because some shred of maternal intuition told her that Gabriel knew she could, and if he hadn't asked her there had to be a reason. Hurt, she'd vowed to talk to him later and find out.

When she did, later that night, he'd explained, "I thought it would make you sad."

And she couldn't lie and say it wouldn't. "But I'd be glad to do it," she'd said. "You don't have to bother Deke."

"He said it wasn't a bother," Gabriel had replied. "He said he'd be honored. He let me use his camera."

She knew that. She'd tried not to notice. She couldn't help it. And nearly every evening since, when Deke got home, he and Gabriel talked serious photography. After dinner Deke put Zack in the backpack and, carrying the little boy, he and Gabriel went out to shoot pictures.

He suggested things for Gabriel to do after school, and every evening they discussed them, too.

"You don't have to spend so much time with him," Erin had told Deke, feeling awkward but obliged to make that clear.

"I *want* to spend time with him. I like him. I hope he likes me." There was an edge to his voice that sounded almost hurt.

"Of course he does. I just—" But she couldn't finish. Her dreams were too muddled. Her hopes had been dashed years ago. And now…now she didn't know what to do.

Friday night Erin thought Deke would be exhausted from the thirty-mile drive to and from Livingston, his long day at the store and from having stopped to see his father, who was two days past his surgery now, recovering well, and already demanding to know what was going on at the store.

She expected he would be happy to collapse on the sofa after dinner and take advantage of Gabriel's being at Mark Nichols's house that evening and thus unable to talk photography.

Instead after they'd finished supper and dishes, Deke had looked around the room and said hopefully, "Who wants to go sledding?"

"Me!" cried Nicolas.

"Moi, aussi," shrilled Sophie.

"Meeee!" crowed Zack, who didn't have a clue. He just wanted to do what the bigger kids did.

So Deke bundled up Zack and Sophie and Nicolas, pulled on jackets and mittens and hats and got ready to go to Sutter's Hill.

"Aren't you coming?" Deke said, clearly surprised when Erin made no move to accompany them.

She shook her head. "I don't think so. I've got these—" she waved a hand toward the heaps of sheets she had volunteered to turn into angel costumes for the pageant in two weeks' time "—to work on."

"Oh, Mama, come," Sophie pleaded.

And Nicolas hopped from one foot to the other. "Come on, Mama. You'd have fun."

Erin, looking at their shining eager faces, knew she would—and knew just as certainly how dangerous to her emotional health that would be. And so once more she shook her head firmly. "Duty calls."

"Is that what it is?" Deke said, challenging her over the tops of the children's heads. "I thought you were just chicken."

Then he opened the door, and they all scampered out, leaving Erin to fume indignantly as she watched them head up the street.

Sutter's Hill, which sat behind Artie Gilliam's house, had been the town sledding spot for as long as Elmer had been a town. Everybody came to Sutter's, young and old alike, because it was fun. There was a long, reasonably swift slope that angled in one direction, and a gentle shorter hill that ended in Gilliam's backyard.

"Somethin' for everyone," Artie always said. And afterward, he and his late wife, Maudie, had always invited everyone in for coffee and cocoa and Maudie's wonderful cookies. It was a town tradition. In fact, even ranch kids and their parents, who could have sledded on any of a dozen places in their own backyards, so to speak, came to Sutter's just because their friends were there, because everyone liked to visit, because it was more fun at Sutter's than anywhere else.

Erin was sure it was still fun, though she doubted Artie was doing the coffee, cocoa, cookies bit anymore. He was, after all, ninety-odd years old now, and Jace and Celie Tucker were living with him. She was sure Celie, who had only finished cutting hair at the Spa at six, wasn't likely to be entertaining sledders all evening.

Picking up the angel costume, Erin determinedly set to work.

She should have accomplished much more than usual, being alone in the house. There were no distractions, no questions from the kids, no conversation from Deke. Only Sammy the dog and Minou the cat distracted at all—if you could call feeding them and putting Sammy out once distractions.

She was more distracted by her thoughts. She kept remembering earlier visits to Sutter's. More often than not she and Taggart had done their sledding at home. But sometimes they'd been able to come with their parents to Sutter's on snowy days. And it had always been such fun—zipping down the long hill on the bobsled, clinging to each other and shrieking as they'd hurtled along at breakneck speed, or building snow forts in Artie and Maudie's yard and pelting each other with snowballs, or helping the little kids make snowmen and decorating them with Artie's old pipes and funny vegetable noses. She remembered the one with the zucchini nose that she and Deke had made the last winter she was home.

She and Deke…

Because even though Deke had been a Livingston

boy, once he'd come to work on the Joneses' ranch, he, too, had discovered the joys of sledding at Sutter's.

They had come together several times when they'd been in college, whenever Deke had been able to get away from work at the store. She wondered if he'd spent today at the store thinking about Sutter's, about how much fun they'd had there, about the snowmen they'd built and the sled rides they'd taken.

And about the day he'd kissed her.

It had, of course, been purely spontaneous—the product of a hair-raising toboggan ride in which she'd burrowed back against him for dear life as they'd careened down the slope and plowed headlong into a snowbank at the end, tipping and rolling over and over until they came to a stop with Erin pinned beneath him. And the two of them had lain, breathless and laughing, their mouths bare inches apart—until Deke had closed the gap and pressed his lips to hers.

It had been quick and, though fierce, nothing at all like the hungry kisses he had given her last Saturday night. That long-ago kiss hadn't been overtly erotic at all. It had been all enthusiasm and exuberance and the sort of thing a guy did with a girl he'd just tipped into a snowbank.

Yet Erin could taste it still.

She sat motionless at the sewing machine, remembering that ride, savoring it again in her mind and her heart and the pit of her stomach. Remembering the snow as it melted against the back of her neck, remembered the heat of Deke's breath on her cheek, remembered his laughing blue eyes suddenly becoming dark as he'd bent his head and kissed her.

She wet her lips without realizing it. She breathed

quickly, heart pounding with the memory. She pressed hard on the pedal, the material whizzed through her fingers. She'd sewn right through four thicknesses. The wing was now attached to the body in an anatomically impossible place.

"Oh, hell!"

And now she had inches—no, *feet!*—of stitching to unpick and resew. Annoyed, Erin slapped the angel costume down and paced the room. But the room wasn't big enough for her feelings so she prowled the house upstairs and down. She went to the window and saw it was still snowing, let the dog out again and felt the sting of snow on her cheeks and heard the sound of shrieks and laughter all the way from Sutter's Hill.

She had taken the kids sledding herself the week before Thanksgiving, when they'd had a foot of snow. They'd laughed and played and she'd come home happy, more satisfied than ever that she had done the right thing bringing them back to Montana. The next morning she'd had a call from an editor she'd worked with at a magazine in Paris and had told her about the experience, about how it had brought back memories of her own childhood.

And the editor had said, "You must shoot it, Erin. We would love such a nostalgic piece—and the photos. Yes, you would bring life in small-town America to Parisians."

"Maybe," Erin had agreed, though she hadn't been in the mood to shoot any photos then. She'd still been drifting then.

But now…

The shouts and shrieks from Sutter's Hill continued, calling to her, beckoning her. And what would she do if she just stayed home? There would be plenty of opportunity later tonight to unpick that entire seam.

Deke had never seen himself as part of a family.

In fact, he'd resisted the notion for years. But having Zack in his life had forced him to take another look at options, to stop and rethink his priorities. Zack—being a good dad to Zack—was his number one priority.

And after four days in Elmer, playing house with Erin was ranking pretty high on his list, too. He discovered he didn't even mind spending every day in the grocery store when he could come home to Erin. Not that he wanted to do it for the rest of his life, but it was certainly easier to do when he had Erin and the kids to come home to.

She was still a little stiff with him, still a little starchy. She still eyed him warily whenever she thought he wasn't looking—and sometimes, damn it, when she knew he was. But he had faith that deep down she still liked him. She was just afraid of what she thought he expected of her. She still loved her husband. And she wasn't ready to let anyone take his place in her life.

Fair enough. Deke even admired her for it.

She was loyal, his Erin. And stubborn. He knew she had determined not to come sledding with them this evening because she might undermine her own resolve, she might have too good a time. He shook his head, despairing, as he reached the top of the hill, Zack riding on his shoulders, and the toboggan rope in his hand.

"Okay, everybody on." He settled Zack in front with his feet under the curve, then wedged Sophie right behind him, then Nico next, and himself last.

"Give you a shove?" Jace Tucker offered.

Deke nodded. "Appreciate it. Hang on tight," he told the kids.

Jace shoved.

"Whooo-hooo!" they yelled. And then they were sailing down the hillside, swooshing past those climbing for another run, with Sophie shrieking madly, Nico yelling and cheering, and even Zack emitting high-pitched squeals until they cruised to a halt in Artie's backyard.

And Sophie shouted, "Mama! You came!"

And Nico called, "Mama! Did you see?"

And Zack clapped his hands and yelled, "Mama! Mama! Mama!"

That startled Deke as much as seeing the woman Zack was calling. But there she was, laughing, too, and wearing a puffy scarlet down jacket over her jeans and shirt as she stood in the snow taking pictures of them.

The kids bounced off the sled and ran over to her.

"Come on, Mama! Come ride with us!" Nico begged.

"Come on, Mama!" Sophie's cheeks were as red as Erin's jacket as she grabbed her mother's arm to pull her over to the toboggan. *"C'est fantastique!"*

"Mama! Mama! Mama!" Zack kept yelling.

And Deke could tell the moment the words registered. The laughter vanished. And she looked from Zack to him, stricken.

"He's glad to see you," Deke said, trying not to make anything of it, trying to restore her equilibrium, make her glad she'd come.

Erin's smile was wavering as her children dragged her over. "I…I just remembered an editor who asked me for some pictures for a small-town America piece," she said. "Although, the light isn't good. I should do it another time. I—"

"Come on," Deke said to her. "Don't worry about the pictures. Come for a ride with us."

"I don't think—"

"Good. Don't," he said. "Come on." And he scooped Zack up and settled the little boy on his shoulders. "Let's go, gang. One last ride."

Sophie and Nicolas fell in behind him. He didn't look back. But when he heard them telling their mother about their earlier runs, Deke felt a sense of relief. Erin was coming.

"It will be too crowded," she said when they reached the top and the kids settled in again and he motioned her to get on. "I'm just here to take pictures."

"Nonsense," Deke growled. "Here, Celie. Take a picture or two." He took Erin's camera and thrust it at Celie Tucker. Then he took Erin's arm and said, "Move up, guys." Then to Erin, "Get on."

Celie snapped a photo of her glaring at him, and another of her rolling her eyes.

"Nice," Deke said with a grin. "Small-town-American enthusiasm at its best."

Erin gnashed her teeth at him, but finally she got on. And he got on behind her, settled his legs on either side of her, moved forward to press his body tight against her so that her bottom was wedged into the vee of his legs.

Oh, yes. Oh, yes yes yes yes yes.

Deke swallowed hard, cleared his throat. "Ready?"

Good God, he sounded hoarse. His nose was by her ear. Her hair drifted against his cheek. He could smell her shampoo and something else exquisitely, ineffably Erin.

"Give you a push?" one of the teenagers offered.

Deke nodded, felt hands at his back, heard the scrape and screech of the snow underneath and Erin's quick intake of breath—and they were away.

It was a kaleidoscope of mind-blowing sensations— speed and cold, closeness and warmth, exhilaration and desire, shrieks and gasps and murmurs. They flew, they leaned, they curved, they swept. And then they glided to a stop.

"Whoo-whee!" yelled Nicolas.

"It was the best, wasn't it, Mama?" Sophie demanded, turning to look back.

"It was the best," Erin said breathlessly after a moment, and then she turned, too, to look back at Deke. Her eyes shone the way he always remembered Erin's eyes shining. Her lips were as red as her jacket, smiling the way Erin always used to smile at him.

And Deke did what he'd been dying to do for days.

He kissed her.

Chapter 9

It wasn't fair!

If Deke's kiss had been demanding, passionate, hungry, desperate, possessive—any of the above—Erin would have stiffened. Her mind would have shut down. Her mouth would have closed up. Her heart would have been safe.

But it wasn't.

It was joyous, gentle, warm, giving. It was the sort of kiss that was entirely appropriate between friends in public circumstances. There was nothing excessive about it, nothing in it that Erin could instinctively resist. It was brief and spontaneous and—damn it!—it left her wanting more.

Wanting *him!*

It was infuriating.

And yet Erin found that she couldn't be furious.

She couldn't be rude or stiff or rejecting in an effort to protect herself because once he'd kissed her, he didn't push. He pulled back and smiled at her—with his mouth *and* with his eyes. And she thought he looked just a little stunned by it, too.

"I'm glad you came, Erin," he said simply as he climbed off the sled, brushed the snow off and helped her get to her feet, too.

Meanwhile Sophie was looking at them, eyes dancing. *He kissed you!* she mouthed gleefully. And Erin knew what her daughter was thinking, what conclusions she was jumping to, and she shook her head fiercely.

Don't! she wanted to say. *Oh, don't! Don't hope! Don't believe!*

But heaven help her, a tiny part of her determined wall of resistance cracked, and she wanted to believe, too.

She eyed him warily, suspiciously, expecting it was a first move, that next she'd find his arm slung about her shoulders or his fingers wrapping hers. But Deke didn't do anything else. He didn't say anything else. He helped the kids up, he dusted off Zack's jacket, he grinned at Sophie and teased Nicolas. And every once in a while, he smiled at her again.

Nervously Erin found herself smiling back. It would be churlish not to, of course. And how could she turn down Celie's invitation that they stop in and have cocoa and cookies in Artie's kitchen?

And once there, when Celie said, "You and Deke ought to..." and Jace said, "When you and Deke go cut your Christmas tree..." she couldn't just jump in and say that Deke would probably be gone by Christmas and in any case there was no such couple as Deke and her.

So she just listened and nodded and smiled politely and sipped her coffee while Deke bounced Zack on his knee and did the same.

Finally the little boy began to suck his thumb and rub his eyes, and Deke got to his feet. "Reckon I ought to get this feller home and in bed. Thanks a lot," he said to Celie. And to Jace and Artie he said, "I'll see you around."

And right then Erin could have made the point that they weren't a couple. She could have kept her kids with her and stayed to talk to Celie and Jace and Artie. But instead she finished her coffee, and Sophie and Nicolas began pulling on their jackets, and all of them left together.

What was happening? Was she hoping? Daring to dream that Felicity might be right? It was a lot to read into a kiss.

And yet as she walked home with an arm on Sophie's shoulders, Deke at her side and Nicolas running on ahead, it felt right. His kiss, this walk—the whole evening—reminded her not merely of her long-ago dreams, but of her life with Jean-Yves.

It wasn't that she was mistaking him for Jean-Yves, either. Not at all! It was that she felt the same wonderful feeling she'd felt when she was with Jean-Yves—as if they belonged together, as if they were a pair.

How on earth could she hope? He was leaving, for heaven's sake, if not next week, the week after! He'd finish hiring people to work for his dad and he'd be gone. Just like that.

He lived in New Mexico. He had work there, he had land there, he had a life there.

And yet...

Something was stirring within her, hopes she'd determinedly squelched were gamely battling back to life.

No, Erin told herself. *No, no, no. Please God, no.*

She had to stop this!

And yet...

A kiss is just a kiss.

There was, Deke was pretty sure, a song by that title. He could almost hear the melody humming through his mind—along with the very clear knowledge that a kiss like the one he'd shared with Erin tonight wasn't just a kiss at all.

Born of desire and yet wholly spontaneous, a product of both the closeness they'd shared during the ride and the need that had been building in him since he'd seen her again, his kiss had held within it such a complexity of unspoken needs, fears, hopes and desires that Deke couldn't even put a name to them all.

In fact, the simple awareness of how much more it meant than any kiss he'd ever shared with anyone before—even Erin herself—jolted him to the core. Deke had kissed a fair number of women. He'd kissed out of duty and out of passion. He'd kissed artlessly and for effect. He'd kissed as a child and as a man with sex on his mind.

But the kiss he'd given Erin meant more. It spoke to their past and to their present and...and what? Something bigger than that. Something *beyond* that.

Friendship? Well, of course they were friends. Always would be.

This hadn't felt quite like friendship, though. It felt bigger than that. Deeper. It felt like a past, a present *and* a future.

A future with Erin Jones?

Deke lay on his bed and stared at the ceiling and considered that. Surely he wasn't serious. A future with a woman implied commitment. It implied forever. It implied marriage!

He'd foreclosed on the notion of marriage at a very early age. He didn't want a future with any woman. Did he?

Well, he never had before, that was certain. Not even Violet, Zack's mother, had inspired a desire for matrimony. Had he discovered Zack's existence, he would probably have decided to give it a shot. For Zack. Because he would have owed it to Zack.

Duty was something Deke understood. When something was his responsibility, he did it. He was, in that way at least, his father's son.

But what he and Violet would have made of a marriage wasn't something he wanted to contemplate. What they had shared had never gone beyond good times and casual sex. He had no idea if they could have made a marriage last.

What he shared with Erin was so much more.

He thought about this past week, about sharing the house, the meals, the conversation, the children. Somehow it all seemed to work.

He thought about the sled ride tonight. It would have been exhilarating and fun with only Zack, but with Erin and Sophie and Nico it had been so much more. And after, when they'd gone into Artie's, the easy conversation and camaraderie reinforced the feeling that they were a family—that they belonged together. And when they'd walked home afterward, him towing the toboggan with one hand and balancing Zack who was nodding off on his shoulders with the other, and Erin with her arm around Sophie's shoulders while Nico ran on ahead like a boisterous puppy, he remembered drawing a breath and looking around—at the town, at the kids, at Erin—and savoring every moment of it, wanting to hang on to it, be a part of it.

He'd never thought about being part of a family— about being a husband, a father. All he remembered of his own family life was the tension between himself and his dad, his mother's inability to do more than wring her hands, and the unhappiness that seemed to permeate the very air they breathed.

He knew that wasn't the way all families were— he'd seen, of course, families like the Joneses—but he'd always expected that it was inevitable for any family *he* was a part of.

But now, tonight, for the first time he began to wonder if he could make a go of it. He wondered if he could make a go of it with Erin.

And he wondered what Erin would think.

It was beginning to look a lot like Christmas.

All over Elmer twinkly little lights were springing up. Garland was appearing on banisters and fences. The little town library had *The Night before Christmas* on the docket for story hour, and the Laundromat had tinsel strung over the three new dryers. The Busy Bee announced stollen and cranberry cake and mince pie on its menu, and the Dew Drop was sporting a neon reindeer in its window with a very bright red nose indeed.

Even on the other side of the door at Erin's house in The Spa, Celie was playing Christmas music for her customers. Bing Crosby, Jimmy Stewart and the Grinch were the fastest moving videos, and just yesterday Celie had put up a tiny Christmas tree with a string of homemade lights and candy canes and set out a plate of homemade Christmas cookies.

And Erin thought it was time she got ready, too. She'd waited a little after Thanksgiving because she'd been so busy, she'd told herself. But it wasn't entirely that. It was Deke and Zack—having them there, having them be part of her memories of Christmas.

She wasn't sure what she'd thought—that they might leave within a few days, that they might head back to New Mexico, never to return and that would be that. In which case, yes, it would have been smart not to prepare for Christmas until they were gone, so she didn't have more bittersweet memories of Christmas in Elmer to think back on year after year.

But they didn't leave. They were still here. And after going sledding and to Artie's last night, she knew that they were going to be a part of her Christmas memories forever.

She might be able to keep Deke out of her bed, but she'd never be able to keep him out of her heart.

So, if she was going to have memories anyway, Erin decided she'd make them the best possible memories she could. And if she cried about them in years to come, well, there was no help for it. At least she'd be happy now.

So that morning, after Deke left for the store and the older kids left for school, she—and Zack—began to get ready for Christmas, too.

"You probably don't remember your first Christmas," she told him because Zack liked a running commentary whether or not he understood every word. "And you might not remember this one, either. Probably, in fact, you won't. But we'll always remember you."

She took him to Artie's store and bought an evergreen wreath and yards of pine garland and Christmas lights from Jace.

"You want me to carry it home for you?" he asked. "Artie won't mind."

And Erin smiled, loving the small-town consideration as she juggled Zack and her purchases. "That would be great."

There was an underlying motive to his offer, as Erin discovered when they got home. Carrying Erin's purchases meant that Jace got to stop in at The Spa behind the house and eat Christmas cookies and kiss his wife. Watching them together made Erin both smile and ache as she missed the take-it-for-granted closeness that happily married couples had.

She contented herself with kissing Zack, then taking him outside where she hung the wreath on the front door and looped lights and garland along the porch railing. Then, while Zack chased Sammy around in the snow, Erin strung the tiny white lights she'd bought over the two evergreens in the front yard. When she finished she turned the lights on even though it was still daylight. It made things look festive and they would welcome the kids when they came home from school that afternoon.

Then Jace and Celie came out and helped her build

a Zack-size snowman between the trees. The little boy stood by, looking amazed, then laughed delightedly when Erin went inside and came out to wrap a bright red scarf around its neck, stick sunglasses on its face, then add a pine cone nose and a line of red gumdrops for a mouth.

"You like that?" she asked, and sang him "Frosty the Snowman" and twirled him around in the snow.

Then Jace went back to the hardware store, Celie went back to The Spa because her next appointment had appeared, and Erin took Zack in for lunch and then a nap. And while he slept, Erin did more holiday preparation—including all the holiday things her Parisian friends had thought she was crazy to do.

As her friend, Nathalie, always said, "Why would I make wonderful food when I can *buy* it everywhere?"

The trouble had always been, while there were wonderful foods to be bought in Paris, none of them evoked the feelings of home she had so wanted during the holidays. And so every year she'd created her own Montana Christmas alongside their Parisian one.

This afternoon she did it again. She prepared the cookie dough and put it in the refrigerator so the kids could cut out Christmas cookies when they came home from school. When that was done, she began to mix up batches of quick bread—loaf after loaf of cranberry and orange and lemon and cinnamon—then baked it and breathed deeply of the aromas that called to mind Christmases of her childhood. She froze some loaves, sliced others and wrapped still others for gifts to friends and her kids' teachers.

She got out the Christmas candles her mother had sent her and put them on the built-in bookcases in the living room. She added the snow globe she and Jean-Yves had bought in Vienna the first Christmas they were married, and the carved wooden Nativity set her grandfather had whittled when she was a child.

Then she got the box that had the Christmas ornaments in it—another Elmer tradition that her friends had rolled their eyes at. The ornaments were ones that she and the kids had made out of baker's clay and yarn and felt—very amateurish and far from elegant. But they recalled so many wonderful times she happily tolerated a little homemade tackiness to celebrate the joys of their family Christmases together.

She was just getting out the children's stockings when Zack appeared on the stairs, looking sleepy-eyed but intrigued by all these new decorations and by seeing her hanging stockings on the fireplace mantel.

"Ah, Zack, you need a stocking, too, don't you?" Erin said.

He clutched his blanket against his cheek and tipped his head quizzically. "S'ocking?"

"One of these with your name on it," she said, flapping Nicolas's white woolen sock on which she'd embroidered his name in red chain stitch down the side. "So Santa can put presents in it."

She didn't think Zack knew what presents were yet, but she figured he'd learn. And there was still time to make him a stocking like Gabriel's and Sophie's and Nicolas's. And she decided she would—even though he might not be here for Christmas.

If he wasn't, well, then Deke could hang it in their house in New Mexico. Let him look at it Christmas after Christmas. Let him tell Zack tales of Montana, of Elmer, of all of them.

Give Deke a few memories, too.

But she didn't let herself think any more about Deke. Instead she put on some Christmas music and swept Zack up into her arms, waltzing him and his blanket around the living room as she told him about Christmas in Paris.

That's what she was doing when the back door banged open and Nicolas and Sophie burst in.

"Are we goin' to get the tree?" Nicolas demanded.

"When can we cut the tree?" Sophie asked.

Obviously the wreath and garland and Christmas lights had signaled that holiday preparations were finally underway.

"Soon," Erin promised. "Maybe tomorrow. This weekend for sure."

Nicolas found the cookie dough in the refrigerator, and Sophie eyed the cranberry bread.

"Can we have some? Please, Mama?" she said hopefully.

"And can we cut out the cookies?" Nicolas begged. "Please, Mama?"

"Please, Mama?" They chorused together. "Please?"

And Zack joined the chorus, bouncing in her arms and echoing words that Erin heard not only with her ears but with her heart. "Mama," he said patting her cheeks. "Mama, please."

Deke found his butcher on Friday.

The clerks hadn't been too hard to come by— Evelyn's niece Cassie was happy to come in every morning while her daughter was in preschool. And Cassie's friend Julia was coming in on Saturdays, and

Evelyn herself agreed to come an extra two afternoons a week. But finding a butcher had been trickier.

Deke had interviewed half a dozen guys with barely disguised drinking problems, one who couldn't seem to remember what time his interview actually was, three more who didn't seem to know pork from lamb, and a couple of teenagers who thought dropping out of school and working would be a lark.

He could have hired one, he supposed, but chances were his old man would have another heart attack over the quality of work—or lack thereof.

He had just started talking to the latest spotty teenage hopeful when Leo Arbogast stopped in on his way to pick up some venison he stored in the freezer locker that John had in back.

Leo, who was pushing seventy, was a recent widower who had been at loose ends since his wife, Dorothy, died in July.

"There's just so much fishin' a feller can do," he said now, talking to Deke over the whine of the meat saw as Deke cut steaks and tried to interview the spotty teenager at the same time.

"Never thought I'd get enough of it." Leo leaned against the meat counter and chatted on. "But there ain't nobody home now to tell my fish stories to. Huntin' stories neither. Did I tell you 'bout shootin' this buck?"

"You did, Leo," Deke said.

The teenager snapped his gum, glanced at his watch and yawned. Another customer appeared behind the one waiting for the steaks.

"Deke," Evelyn called. "The vegetable shipper's on the phone."

Deke sighed and looked hopefully at the teenager

who was supposed to want this job desperately. The boy looked blankly back.

"Say," Leo said, "you want me to do that?"

Deke finished the cut and looked up. "Do what?"

"I can cut them steaks," Leo offered. "Used to work in a butcher shop years back in Miles City."

"Er," Deke said, staring at Leo, who was looking hopeful as well as helpful. The customer tapped his foot. Evelyn waved the phone at him. "Sure," Deke said. "Why not?"

Half an hour later he had Leo in an apron behind the meat counter, and the spotty teenager was long gone.

It was the answer to a prayer. Leo was in his element, charming the ladies who came for their pork chops or roasts, swapping fishing stories with the men who dropped in for some cold cuts, cutting everything with a lot more expertise than Deke brought to it.

"Well, now," Leo said when they were closing that night, "that was fun." He heaved a satisfied sigh. "You serious about this job?"

Deke nodded. "Absolutely." He was prepared to battle his father over it, though.

"Leo Arbogast? You hired Leo? You're joking." John said half an hour later when Deke stopped by the hospital on his way home.

"I'm not," Deke said stubbornly. "He knows what he's doing and he'll work hard. He's glad to be there. Likes the people. You couldn't get a better man." Not that he expected his father would agree.

John Malone sat silent for a full minute, possibly longer, while Deke tried to anticipate the arguments he'd need. Finally his father just shrugged. "Leo's a good man." He looked away out the window into the winter night. "So," he remarked after a moment, "I reckon you'll be leavin' then."

Leaving?

Deke hadn't even thought about it. But it was what he wanted, wasn't it?

He'd been absolutely clear about that from the very beginning. He would help out because it was necessary. That didn't mean he was staying. He *wasn't* staying. He had a life in New Mexico. He had a home, a career. He had no intention of working in the grocery store for the rest of his life.

And yet now that he could leave, he felt strangely reluctant.

He shifted from one boot to the other and rubbed a hand against the back of his neck, aware that while his father wasn't looking at him directly, he was staring at Deke's reflection in the window glass.

And Deke, feeling his gaze, shrugged irritably. "It's not like I'm sure Leo knows what he's doing. Can't expect Evelyn to ride herd on 'em all."

His father's brows lifted fractionally and he turned his head and looked straight at him now. His chest expanded. His breathing seemed to come a little easier. "Reckon so."

"Besides, you're not out of the hospital yet. If Leo or Evelyn has questions, they can't keep running up here to talk to you, can they? And even when you're home, you're not going to want them pestering you every minute."

Deke was prowling around the room as he spoke, aware of his father's eyes on him, assessing him, aware that riding herd on his father's employees had little to do with what was nagging at him. He couldn't even articulate what was. He jammed his hands into the pockets of his jeans and hunched his shoulders as he paced. When he reached the end of the room, he spun around. He could settle part of the issue now. "Unless you want me gone," he challenged his old man.

They stared at each other. The old man, the young man. The hidden agendas neither would speak.

Finally, slowly, almost imperceptibly, John Malone shook his head. "Stay as long as you want."

Hardly a welcome. But a damn sight closer to one than what he'd got when he'd arrived at Thanksgiving.

Deke almost smiled. But he wasn't sure there was that much to smile about. Not yet. Instead he gave one quick, jerky nod of his head. "Well, fine. That's settled, then."

"Deke! Deke! Didja see the lights?"

"Deke! Look! We made cookies! You can have an angel or a snowman or a tree!"

"Deke! How do you shoot Christmas lights at night?"

"Da-ad! Cookie?"

The kids swooped down on him like a pack of boisterous puppies the minute Deke opened the back door. They'd been watching out the window for his truck for the past half hour.

"He'll be here. Relax," Erin told them over and over. But deep down she was almost as eager as they were to have him home. A mistake, she assured herself. But knowing that it was and being able to do something about it were two different things.

"I saw the lights," Deke said. He was grinning as he shed his jacket. It had started to snow about an hour ago, and there was a light dusting on it and on his hat.

He hung them up and then reached down to scoop Zack up in his arms. "The lights are terrific," he told Nicolas. "I could see 'em almost as soon as I turned off the highway. Like beacons guiding me home." He lifted his gaze from Nico's and met Erin's, and there was a warmth in his eyes that made her heart kick over.

Sophie shoved a plate of the cookies at him and he admired them. "Great cookies. Do I get to eat 'em or are they just for looking at?"

Sophie giggled. "You can eat them. I made the angels. Have an angel."

"How about after dinner? Don't want to spoil my appetite. It smells so darn good." Another quick smile in Erin's direction and a deep sigh of appreciation. "And we'll go out and try to shoot the lights after dinner, too, okay?" he said to Gabe, who nodded.

Then Deke turned to his son. "Did you make cookies today, buddy?"

And Zack bounced in his arms and nodded, beaming and pointing at the plate Sophie held. "Cookies! Mama cookies."

Mama? Once more Deke's eyes sought Erin's.

She felt her cheeks burn and quickly she shook her head. "I didn't teach him that. He just hears what the other kids call me." She certainly didn't want Deke thinking she was getting ideas. "Come and eat," she said now. "Dinner's ready." She motioned everyone to sit down.

They all sat and began passing dishes. She'd made chili and salad and had sliced up some of the bread she'd baked earlier. Deke filled a bowl with chili and another with salad, took a bite and smiled blissfully. "Terrific. Thank you."

"You're welcome. How'd things go today? How's your dad?"

"Doing pretty well, I think. Sitting up. Bossing nurses and my mom." He flashed her a conspiratorial grin. "But amazingly enough he was actually satisfied with the butcher I hired."

Erin's stomach turned to lead. "You hired a butcher?"

She knew that almost right away Deke had found two young women to work as checkers and stockers along with Evelyn, his dad's old standby. But from everything he'd said, he hadn't found a good butcher. They were either too inexperienced or too incompetent or too untrustworthy or something. And though she'd never admitted it—even to herself—she'd been glad to hear it. She hoped he'd take his time, hoped that he wouldn't find one. Not for a while at least. As long as he didn't find a butcher, he wouldn't leave.

But now he had.

Erin paused, her fork halfway to her mouth, and mustered a smile. "Really? Who is it? Do I know him?"

"Leo Arbogast."

She knew Leo. "I remember his wife more than him. Dorothy substitute taught up here when I was in high school. So, Leo's doing it?" That pretty much clinched the leaden stomach feeling. Leo Arbogast wasn't going to turn out to be a dud. He'd be there, rain or shine, and he'd get the job done.

Apparently Deke thought so, too. He nodded happily. "Came in to pick up some venison from his locker today—and ended up working the rest of the afternoon. Dad's pretty pleased."

"I'll bet. So," she said cautiously, "that's all, then?"

She tried to make her voice sound perky and upbeat. "All the people you're hiring, I mean?"

Deke nodded. "That's all. Zack, stop that. No throwing lettuce. Gabe, pass me a napkin. Did you try shooting the shadows like I told you?"

And that was the end of that. The conversation moved on. Deke said nothing else about the hiring he'd done. Nothing else about the grocery store at all. Or about his father. He talked to Gabriel about the shots he'd suggested Gabriel try. And he ate cookies—five of them—one each of the cutout figures that Sophie made. Then after dinner, Nicolas dragged him into the living room to admire candles and the snow globe and the stockings that were hanging from the mantel.

"Mama's making Zack one," Nicolas told Deke. "Just like ours."

"Because every boy should have a stocking," Erin said quickly. "To take wherever he goes." In case Deke thought she was angling to hang another one on their mantel and make them stay.

"Do you have time to do that?" he asked doubtfully.

"Of course I have time."

Her annoyance must have been apparent because he took a step back and raised his hands, palms outward. "I was only askin'. I don't expect—"

"I know you don't expect. I *want* to do it. For Zack."

He nodded. "Of course. For Zack."

They stared at each other for a long moment. Erin, who had never had any trouble reading Deke's expressions before, found him inscrutable now.

"Can we go shoot lights?" Gabriel asked.

Deke turned. "Sure. Let's." He got his camera and, hoisting Zack into his arms, he followed Gabriel out of the house without looking back. Nicolas, bouncing puppy-like, went too.

"Are you going to hem my angel costume, Mama?"

"What? Oh, yes." Erin turned away from the window and shoved a hand through her hair as she smiled at her daughter. "Good idea. We'll do it now."

"And then if you show me how, maybe can I do a little of the embroidery on Zack's stocking?" Sophie said eagerly.

"Of course." Erin smiled. "That would be nice."

She spent the rest of the evening busy with Sophie, always aware of Deke in the background, hearing his deep voice as he talked to the boys or played with Zack, memorizing the sound of it, knowing it wouldn't be long now.

But he didn't say anything. It was like waiting for the other shoe to drop.

It wasn't until later, after all her kids had gone to bed and she was embroidering the *A* in Zack's name on his stocking, that Deke came downstairs and wandered into the living room. She knew he'd just finished reading to Zack and putting him down. It was a time she ordinarily cherished—the few minutes a day when they would have a cup of coffee or tea together and talk about the day.

But tonight she wished she didn't have to listen. She didn't want to hear what he was going to say.

"Coffee?" he said. "Or tea?"

"I'm pretty tired," she said, setting down the stocking. "Maybe I'll just go up now." *Put off the inevitable.*

"Oh, come on. You can't be that tired. You've only decorated an entire house, baked several thousand cookies, a dozen loaves of bread, outfitted a choir of angels and supervised an almost-two-year-old all day. How can you possibly say you're tired?" He was grinning at her.

And Erin couldn't help smiling back. Damn, damn, damn. "Fine," she said, giving in. "Tea, please."

He went into the kitchen and put on the kettle, then came back into the living room. She was used to him sitting in the leather armchair next to the fireplace. But tonight he didn't sit down, he prowled around the room, shoved his hands in the back pockets of his jeans, prowled some more. Then he hunkered down and poked at the fire in the fireplace. When the kettle whistled, he jumped up again.

"I'll get it."

Erin poked the needle in and out of the wool of the stocking and felt increasing dread. Just say it, she told him silently. Get it over with. Tell me you're going to leave.

He came back with the tea and handed her a cup, then, carrying his, prowled some more. He picked up the snow globe and stared at it. It was the Riesenrad, the giant Ferris wheel in Vienna, and she and Jean-Yves had seen it snow like that in Vienna just like it was snowing now as Deke tipped it and watched the flakes come down.

"Doesn't snow that much in Santa Fe," he said after a while. "Can't count on a white Christmas."

"Or in Paris, either," she agreed. "I loved it there. But it's nice to be here where snow is pretty much a given."

"Yeah."

"Not that it can't be nice elsewhere," she added

quickly, determined again that he wouldn't think she was trying to make him stay.

"Never celebrated much before," Deke said, still studying the globe. "Not much point—just me."

"Well, you have Zack now."

"Yeah." He glanced her way. "Thanks for bein' so good to him—and for including him. And for his stocking and all."

"I'm glad to. I told you. You can hang it for him every year—no matter where you are." There. That was as close as she could come.

Deke nodded, one corner of his mouth lifting. "He'll like that." He set down the globe and went to stand with his back to the fireplace. He cradled the mug in his hands. "He likes it here."

Erin looked up. The needle stilled in her hand. "We've enjoyed having him."

He nodded and rocked back on his heels. "I don't know if he'll even remember it. But he might. I'd...like him to have the memories."

Unsure she was following him, Erin didn't say a word.

"I kind of have to keep an eye on things at the store," he said hurriedly. "I'm pretty sure Leo will work out well, and the girls, too. But my dad isn't even out of the hospital yet. And my mom would like it if Zack was around and—" he raked a hand through his hair "—I wondered if you'd mind putting up with us a while longer?"

"Longer?" Erin faltered. Her heart had skipped a beat.

"Till after Christmas?" Deke said. "I know it's a lot longer than you expected. It's a real imposition. But

Zack's so happy. He's settled in. And it would be really good to have the holiday here."

Her heart was beating steadily again. Fast. Eagerly. More happily than she could have imagined. "You want to stay?" She was smiling now, dancing inside. *Fool,* she called herself. *You're just delaying the inevitable.*

But if it was true, she didn't care. He was staying through Christmas!

He nodded. "If you're sure you don't mind?"

Erin smiled and shook her head. "I don't mind at all."

Chapter 10

It was the holiday season of her youthful dreams—she and Deke together, children chattering around them as they went up to the ranch to cut a Christmas tree on Sunday afternoon.

Erin hadn't expected him to come along. It was the only day of the week he didn't have to work at the store and could do what he wanted to do. She thought he might take Zack and go see his sister or something. She was very careful to assure him that he didn't have to come on the Christmas tree expedition.

"Not come?" Deke frowned. "Why wouldn't I?"

"I don't know. I thought maybe you might want a little time on your own. Away from the store. Away from the kids."

"Away from the store, yes." Deke agreed with that wholeheartedly. "But not the kids. Or you."

Or you.

He didn't come down with both feet on the words. He didn't give her a lascivious wink or a come-hither leer. If he had, Erin thought in a moment of honesty, she might well have run in the other direction. But his casual inclusion of her made her smile. And on top of the kiss he'd given her on Friday night...

Don't, she warned herself. *Do not get your hopes up.*

And she wasn't—*really* she wasn't. She was just going to enjoy the afternoon, just going to enjoy the whole holiday season. Nothing wrong with that.

So right after lunch they all clambered into Deke's truck and set off for the ranch. Gabriel brought his camera, Deke brought his, and Erin couldn't resist bringing hers along, too. The photos she'd taken of their sledding experience had turned out wonderfully. She had found herself looking at them over and over, staring at the pictures of Deke and Zack, of Deke and her kids. Of Deke.

She had even framed one of them—of all of them on the toboggan. She told herself she picked the one she did because it was good of Sophie and Nicolas. But if she was honest, she picked the one where it was good of all of them—but best of Deke. Whenever she looked at it, she simply couldn't keep her eyes off Deke.

She kept it on her dresser next to the one of Jean-Yves and Gabriel as they'd come up the walk that afternoon almost three years ago. And every night she looked at the photos before she went to bed. She smiled a little and felt sad a little.

"Life goes on," Jean-Yves always said. It was what had got him through the hardest parts of his job. It was what had got her through his death. "You can't hang on to the past," he had told her years ago when she had told him about her unrequited love of Deke.

"Do you hope to go back to him in the future?" he'd asked her.

And she'd shaken her head. "No." There had been no point. No chance of that.

"Then you must go forward," he said simply. "You must make the most of what you have."

I'm trying, she told him every night when she looked at his picture. *I'm trying hard.*

And sometimes—like today—it was easy.

It had been a long time since she'd cut a tree for Christmas. She wasn't even sure where to go. But a phone call to Taggart this morning had solved the problem.

"You can come with us, if you want," he'd said. "We're going out this afternoon, too."

But Erin had declined. "No, I think you'd better send us in the entirely opposite direction. It wouldn't help family relations if both of us settled on the same tree."

"We wouldn't," Taggart said. "You can't get two people to agree on the same tree, let alone nine!"

"Eleven," Erin corrected. "Deke and Zack are coming, too."

"Oh, yeah? He's still with you? Hey, Felicity," he called to his wife, "I think you might be right."

"About what?" Erin demanded.

"She said she thought Deke might hang around awhile."

Erin thought there was a good possibility that Felicity had said a great deal more than that, but she wasn't sure she wanted to hear her sister-in-law's speculations.

"Deke is staying until after Christmas," she informed

her brother. "He's hired some new employees at the store and he has to make sure they work out. Besides, his father isn't out of the hospital yet. He can't leave until someone can manage things. And in her condition, along with C.J. and the job with Poppy, Milly certainly can't. Besides, he wanted Zack to have a family Christmas."

"A lot of reasons," Taggart said. But even so, she could hear the tolerant amusement in his tone.

"Just tell me where we can go to find a tree," she said irritably.

Taggart laughed, but in the end he told her.

"Thank you."

"Anytime," he said. Then as she was about to hang up, he said, "Erin?"

She felt instantly wary. "What?"

"Deke's a good guy. I hope—" Taggart paused, then found the words he was looking for "—I hope things work out the way you want them to."

"Thanks, Taggart," she said softly. "I do, too."

Deke wasn't much used to family outings. In his family going "out" meant getting away from everyone else. No, it meant getting away from his father. Warm family feelings weren't thick on the ground.

But he'd had new family experiences ever since he and Zack had moved in with Erin. And cutting down the tree wasn't something he intended to miss.

The area that Taggart sent them to was an area Erin said she remembered well from their childhood expeditions in search of trees. Deke thought she would find one, then say, "This is it," and he would cut it down and they would head home.

In fact, everyone had an opinion and wasn't afraid to voice it. He balanced Zack on his shoulders and followed the rest of them over the snowy hillside.

"How about this one? No, this one?" Nicolas had a hundred opinions that changed by the second as he bounded on ahead.

Sophie was nearly as bad. She kept wandering off and calling, "Over here! I've found the perfect one over here!"

And then when they would all get there, she would have changed her mind or one of her brothers would point out the "perfect tree's" drawbacks: it was too short, too tall, too fat, too lopsided.

Erin was more thoughtful, but she tended to find trees she thought needed tender, loving care. "We could turn the bad side to the wall," she'd say whenever Gabriel pointed out a gaping hole to her.

"We could leave it here to live out its natural life in peace," Gabe said.

And by then Nicolas would have found another one and they would trundle on. Eventually it became such a joke that Gabe started taking pictures of the "perfect trees."

"I'm going to do a gallery of them," he said, eyes laughing.

And Deke laughed, too, because it was a good idea and because it was a memory he would love to see preserved on film. Mostly it was the feeling he wanted to preserve—this feeling that you could each have your own opinion and be teased about it and no one would get upset.

"What do you think?" Erin asked him.

"I think this is wonderful," he said quite honestly.

She blinked. "What's wonderful?" She looked around and he realized she was looking for a tree.

He shook his head. "Not a tree. This. Doing this. All of us. I like it."

"Oh." The notion seemed first to startle her, then to please her. She smiled at him with such warmth that it curled his toes inside his hiking boots. "Me, too."

A strand of dark hair was blowing across her face just then, and automatically he reached out and brushed it away. His glove touched her skin—not even his fingers—but it was enough to make him want more. To want to take her hand in his and walk with her.

They stood, staring at each other. Then—whap!—a snowball hit him in the back.

"Gotcha!" Nicolas yelled.

Deke swung Zack down and handed him to Erin. "Sorry. Do you mind? Business to attend to."

And, turning swiftly, he scooped up a handful of snow and went after Nico.

He hadn't had a snowball fight in years. It was wonderful, exhilarating as, yelling and chortling, he and Nico and Gabe and Sophie pounded each other with snowballs. Looking up to see Zack waving his hands in glee and Erin laughing delightedly was one more thing to savor.

Finally, when Nico had called truce and they were all damp and covered with snow, anyway, Erin showed them how to make snow angels.

"See," she said to Zack, helping him flop on his back in the deep snow and waggle his arms up and down, "You're making wings. You're the littlest angel." She took his hands and lifted him carefully out of the snow, then turned to show him the pattern he'd made.

Zack was delighted. "Dad!" he yelled. "See me angel!"

"The only time you'll ever be one," Deke told him with a grin.

Erin laughed. "He's always an angel for me."

"I doubt that," Deke said gruffly.

Erin nuzzled the little boy's neck, making him giggle. "We get along, don't we, Zack?"

That much was abundantly clear. Zack had bonded with Erin and with her kids. Deke felt like he had a bond with her kids, too. And with her. Well, of course he did. But what did it mean?

What did he want it to mean?

He was still puzzling that over, standing there staring down the hill when something occurred to him, and he said, "What about that one?"

"What? What one?" Erin looked at him oddly.

Deke pointed. "That tree." He was the only one—besides Zack—who hadn't suggested a tree so far. He hadn't intended to at all. He'd just come along for the ride. It hadn't seemed to be his place to suggest anything. But he and Zack were now a part of this—they'd been included. And he had as good an eye as anyone, didn't he?

Now he waited for the inevitable choruses of "It's too fat" and "It's too crooked" and "It's too tall" and "It's got a hole in this side."

But nobody said a word. They all fanned out, moved closer, walked around it. The tree Deke had spotted was about ten feet tall—a good height for the very high-ceilinged rooms of Erin's house. It was full but not so bushy you couldn't hang anything on it. It didn't seem to have any gaps the size of the Grand Canyon anywhere in it. It was, to his mind, the perfect tree.

Which meant, if Deke were honest, that it was exactly the sort of tree he'd always wanted to have for Christmas in their house when he was growing up.

Of course they'd never had one like it. His father had said big trees were too much bother. His mother said they were messy and hard to clean up afterward. They'd always had a small tabletop tree decorated with those glass ball ornaments that broke if you looked at them—especially when you were eight. Their trees had always been very pretty, but not very touchable.

"Why ever would you want to touch a tree?" his mother had asked when he'd said that once.

"It's pretty big," he hedged now. "It'd probably be a pain to drag down the hill. Might be too big for where you want to put it."

Erin didn't answer. She was still circling the tree thoughtfully. So were the kids.

"Hmm," Sophie said, pursing her lips.

"Umm," Nicolas said hopping around it, studying it from all angles.

"Ah," Gabriel said, looking at it through the camera lens, snapping the shutter, moving on, shooting again.

"Tree?" Zack said hopefully.

"There's a lot of other trees," Deke said.

"No," Erin said flatly. "This is the one."

"Yea!" The kids all cheered and bobbed their heads and nodded.

"It's not too tall?" Deke said, feeling suddenly unsure. "You don't think it'll be too big? Dwarf the living room? What if there aren't enough lights? What about ornaments? It'll take a ton."

"Then we'll make more. Or find some."

"But—"

"It's perfect, Deke," Erin said, eyes shining as she smiled at him.

It was right about then, Deke knew he was in love with Erin Jones.

He pushed the broom around the grocery store the following evening and, as he had all day, thought about Erin. More specifically about *loving* Erin.

In some ways, he rationalized, he had loved her for years. Certainly, back before she'd left for Paris and he'd left for New Mexico, she'd been the most significant woman in his life, the one who mattered most, who knew him best. And naturally he'd felt a love for her that a guy feels for a dear, devoted friend.

And back then—other than the physical sort of back seat groping he did with his assorted girlfriends—that was the only kind of love he'd been capable of.

The other kind—the soul-deep, heart-searing, mind-warping sort that his sisters seemed to have found with their husbands and Taggart had found with Felicity and, let's face it, that Erin had found with Jean-Yves—had been out of his league entirely.

And now?

Now he understood its power. Now he saw its value. Now he believed in it and wanted it—with Erin.

He'd gone to bed last night distracted by the realization that he loved her, trying to make sense of what that meant, trying to figure out which way to run with it. It wasn't a foregone conclusion, he feared. It might have been if he'd fallen in love with Erin fifteen years ago. But not now.

Now they were adults. Now they each had a life, commitments, children.

What did it mean to love Erin? What did that love ask of him?

And what was he going to ask of her?

And that's where his head had been all day long—fretting about what he would be asking, and if she could give it. Whether or not she loved him. Or was she still in love with Jean-Yves?

It always came back to Jean-Yves.

She was still his friend, he didn't doubt that. But could she ever be more than that?

She slept with you, idiot! he told himself over and over.

And that might have convinced him that she loved him—*if* she'd wanted to keep sleeping with him. But she hadn't. In fact, she'd made a big point, when he'd come and asked if he and Zack could stay with her, about providing him room in her house—but not in her bed. Once had apparently been enough, Deke thought grimly.

A guy could have some serious doubts about his prowess as a lover given enthusiasm like Erin's.

The only thing that saved him there was remembering that, at the time, his lovemaking hadn't left her cold. Either he'd given her pleasure or she'd sure as shootin' faked it. And this was Erin, he reminded himself. Erin would never fake a thing like that.

No. He was pretty sure he'd pleased her. But afterward she hadn't been so pleased—and that was what bothered him. Afterward, she'd acted as if making love with him had been a betrayal of her love for her husband.

And there he was, back thinking about bloody Jean-Yves LaChance again—and he was no further along thinking about what he was going to do about Erin.

"Hey, Deke, I'm off now." Leo came out of the back room, pulling on his jacket, smiling as brightly as he had been when he'd arrived that morning.

Deke couldn't help smiling back. "Go okay today?" he asked. It had seemed so to him. Having Leo there had made things run a lot smoother. But he hadn't asked Leo before now.

"Fantastic." Leo's grin widened further. "Time flies when you're havin' fun."

Deke raised his eyebrows. "Fun?"

"All in how you look at it," Leo said. "Helluva lot more fun bein' here workin' and visitin' with folks than it has been sittin' at home."

Leo was right, Deke thought. The grocery store wasn't a bad place. It was a lot easier to deal with now than it had been when he'd looked at it from the perspective of a twenty-two-year-old. Then he could only see it as a millstone around his neck. It amazed him that his father, who'd been even younger than he was when he'd gone to work with his father, had taken to it so easily.

"See you in the morning," Leo said. "If you stop and see your old man, tell him I'll look in on him soon."

"I'll do that."

It was nearly six-thirty, and he really didn't want to stop at the hospital. He wanted to get home to see Erin and the kids. But he knew his father counted on the daily report.

* * *

"You're late," his father said when Deke walked into his room. He was sitting up in bed, wearing a robe. His color was better now. His voice was stronger. And apparently so were his opinions.

Deke ignored the comment. "Leo's working out fine. He said he'd stop and see you soon."

"Not here he won't."

Deke just looked at him, not sure what he was supposed to say to that.

"I mean," his father announced, "I'm going home tomorrow." There was a note of triumph in his voice. He looked like he might actually smile. Of course he didn't.

"Well, that's good," Deke said. "Glad to hear it. Doc must think you're doing well."

"Doc wants this bed for some other poor sod," his father said. "But I'm not sad to be going home." He let out an expressive sigh, then fixed Deke with a steady stare. "What'd you decide?"

Deke frowned. "About what?"

"What you were rattlin' on about last time you were in here," John Malone said impatiently. "Whether you were stayin' or goin'."

"Staying," Deke said. "For now."

His father frowned. "What's that mean? For now? Till tomorrow? Till next week?"

"Till after Christmas. At least."

His father's look still challenged him, but Deke had no further answer than that. So he just shrugged. "That's all I know. Do you need help getting home tomorrow?"

"Of course I don't. And you'll be workin' anyway."

"Right. Of course you don't." Deke rubbed a hand against the back of his neck, wondering why he bothered and wanting perversely to laugh at the same time. "Well, fine. I'll drop by the house tomorrow night after work and see you there. Wish Mom the joy of you," he muttered under his breath.

John frowned. "What's that you say?"

"Nothing, Dad. Have a good night. See you tomorrow." Deke started for the door.

"You haven't brought the boy yet," his father called after him.

"I will." He would sometime. But he needed to sort out his own life first.

"Dad wants me to bring Zack to see him," he said that night at the dinner table. It was, he discovered, easier to talk about his father than to sort out his own life. Much easier than discussing what mattered—which was how he felt about Erin and how she felt about him.

"Does he?" Erin raised a brow. "That's good, surely. And you wouldn't have to stay long. They don't like little kids in hospitals for more than a few minutes."

"He's not going to be in the hospital. He's coming home tomorrow."

"He must be doing well. I'm sure he'll be glad to get home."

"Drive my mother nuts," Deke muttered, then sighed. "Guess I'll take him over on Sunday. Can't do it during the day. I'd be missing work. God help us, the store might fall apart if I missed five minutes there."

"I could take him," Erin offered.

Deke paused, his fork halfway to his mouth. "Take Zack to my folks'? You'd do that?"

"Sure. Why not?"

"You know what he's like."

"With you." Erin shrugged. "He's not that way with me."

"He could be." Deke had never told her the disparaging things his father had said about her "leading him astray" all those years ago.

"I suppose he could. But he won't. He's always polite," Erin said, then grinned. "Maybe he just thinks of me as a potential customer. We could stop by tomorrow afternoon."

"We could make a Welcome Home sign!" Nicolas suggested. And when both adults stared at him, he bounced eagerly on his chair as he explained to Deke, "We did that for my dad when he came home from the hospital once. And for a friend of Mama's. Mama says it always makes people feel better, don't you?" He looked at his mother for confirmation.

"Well, yes, but…" Erin looked slightly stunned at the notion, but she seemed actually to be considering it. And the longer she sat there, considering, the more intrigued she looked. Finally she smiled across the table at Deke, and he felt that current of awareness arc between them again. "That's not a bad idea, actually."

"A Welcome Home sign? Pardon my skepticism." Anyone less likely to inspire Welcome Home signs than John Malone was hard to imagine.

"Why not make one?" Erin said, actually looking enthused. "I'll bet no one ever has."

"You'd win that bet," Deke said dryly.

She rolled her eyes at him. "Well, I think Nicolas has a good idea. It might make your father happy. And even if he isn't, what do we have to lose but some time and some butcher paper? And we've got a roll of that."

"He'll think it's a waste," Deke said. He knew his old man.

"He'll think we care," Erin countered.

"Do you?"

She stared at him, as if his question surprised her. Then she said, "Of course we do. He's your father!"

Which meant what? That she cared about his father because she cared about him? Deke wished he knew, but he couldn't bring himself to ask. She would simply say that of course she cared about him. They were friends, weren't they?

And yes, damn it, they were. But Deke didn't want simply to be friends! He wanted more. He looked at Erin with a mixture of anguish and frustration.

She got up and started clearing the table. "I'll make room," she said to the kids.

"I'll get the paper," Sophie said, leaping up.

"I'll get the markers," said Gabriel, shoving back his chair.

"I'll find the glitter." Nicolas rushed off.

Markers? Glitter? John Malone?

"It'll be *trop* cool, you'll see," Nicolas said cheerfully over his shoulder.

"*Trop* cool?" Deke echoed.

"Don't worry," Erin said. She touched his shoulder as she passed. And when he looked up she smiled at him. "It will be fine, Deke."

And then, by God, she bent and kissed his cheek!

Deke spotted the Welcome Home sign flapping from the porch roof of his parents' house as he drove up the following evening.

A twelve-foot-long, three-foot-high swath of butcher

paper proclaimed WELCOME HOME in multicolored markers, with BIENVENUE written beneath it in neon orange and pink and green, so it could be read, as well, by any French-speaking citizens of Livingston.

"You never know who might see it," Erin had said with a shrug last night. "I don't really think it matters, do you?"

Deke hadn't been thinking much all day—except about Erin having kissed him!

Had it been a "friendly" kiss? Or something more?

She'd breezed out of the room before he could do more than sit bolt upright in response. And when she'd come back from the kitchen, she'd been talking to the kids about the banner, as if she'd never given the kiss another thought.

Probably she hadn't, damn it! Deke didn't know what to think. It had been all he could do not to keep touching the spot, like some goofy, besotted teenager.

Now as he pulled up in front of the house and could read the sign in the yard light as bright as day, he tried to imagine what his father must have thought upon seeing it there. Probably that they'd come to the wrong house.

Grinning, he got out of the truck. As he got closer he could see that each individual letter had been colored in with small seasonal drawings: wreaths and Christmas trees, candy canes and snowmen, and—Deke laughed when he saw them—doves of peace.

Dealing with John Malone, they'd need all the doves of peace they could get.

Erin's Suburban was parked across the street, and Deke wondered what time she'd got there. What had happened to her "quick visit"? Maybe she'd hung the banner earlier and had come back just a little while ago to make an appearance with the kids. That seemed likely.

So maybe he could drop in, congratulate his father on getting home, suffer the daily grilling about the store and then he and Erin could make a getaway together.

But when he opened the door it didn't sound like anyone was going anywhere at all—not soon at least.

"Oh, good, Deke. You're here." His mother beamed at him as she crossed the hall from the kitchen to the family room, carrying a covered dish. "We're just getting ready to eat. In here—with John. He said we should all come in there. Erin brought dinner. Wasn't that lovely of her? And the sign! Did you see the sign she and the children made? John was thrilled."

Thrilled? It didn't sound like his father. And he wanted them all to eat with him in the family room? That didn't sound like his father, either.

Scratching his head, Deke went to investigate. He knew Cash had brought down a bed from upstairs and had put it in the family room so their dad wouldn't have to climb the stairs. Deke had envisioned his father ruling his castle from there—like a king directing his servants, the way he had bossed everyone from his hospital bed.

But at the moment he looked less like a king than like the ringmaster of a three-ring circus. He was in bed, all right, but hardly in regal splendor.

While Deke's mother had obviously decorated the house for Christmas—the perfect tiny tree was sitting on the table under the window, the angel choir of candles sat on the buffet and the requisite sprig of

mistletoe hung in the doorway just as he remembered—
nothing else was at all the same.

His mother was setting up a buffet line of sorts on the
parson's table in the family room. Gabriel was opening
up TV trays, while keeping an eye on the action in a
hockey game on television. Sophie was sitting on the
edge of John Malone's bed showing him an album of
photos and talking nineteen to the dozen, and Nicolas
and Zack were sprawled on their stomachs on the floor,
coloring on another giant piece of paper.

Deke's father, amazingly enough, seemed to be
taking it all in stride.

He had an eye on the hockey game, like Gabe. He
was listening to Sophie and paging through the album
with her. And every once in a while he would lift his
gaze in the direction of Nico and Zack. He barely
noticed when Deke walked in.

It was Zack who bounced up and came running.
"Daaaaad!"

"Hey, there!" Deke swept the little boy up in his arms
and gave him a fierce hug, aware as he did so that his
father's eyes had settled on him. Judging him. At least,
that's what it felt like. He didn't look John's way. Instead
he tickled Zack's belly. "Whatcha doin', buddy?"

"Picture," Zack told him. "Big picture!" He lifted his
arms and spread them wide, like the sun coming up.

"You makin' a picture for me?"

Zack shook his head. "Pa," he said and pointed at
his grandfather.

Deke blinked. "You're making a picture for Grandpa?"

Zack nodded emphatically. "Yep, Pa," he agreed,
then wriggled to get down. "Nico me." He pointed to
the picture, which was pretty much nonrepresentational

as far as Deke could tell. But what Zack lacked in skill he made up for in intensity as he flopped down beside Nicolas and began coloring furiously once more.

"It's a Christmas picture," Nico explained. "'Cause Zack's grandpa says they need a Christmas picture. See. I'm doing a tree an' angels an' Jesus an' the sheep, an' Zack is doin' the sky. Zack's grandpa liked the banner. He said me an' Zack have talent."

"Did he?" Deke looked at his father, surprised.

His father stared back as if daring him to dispute it.

Deke didn't. He just nodded. "He's right," he told Nicolas.

"Hi." Erin's voice made Deke spin around.

She was standing right behind him, bearing a plate of roast, carrots and potatoes. And her smile was enough to make his heart kick over in his chest.

"Hi, yourself." He almost stumbled over his boots trying to get out of her way. And when she had to slide past him to get to the table, their bodies brushed, and he felt like a teenager all over again.

He cleared his throat. "You brought dinner, Ma said?" He nodded at the platter.

"I decided it would be easier. Give your mom a little break." She set the platter on the table.

"That was, um, nice of you." Cripes, he sounded like an idiot. "I'm...sure she appreciates it."

"We both appreciate it," his father said gruffly.

That surprised Deke, too. But the old man was almost smiling. He asked Deke what he thought of that banner, had he ever seen such an amazing banner, and his chest had almost puffed with pride.

He seemed happier than Deke had seen him in years.

He was still taciturn and given to the occasional gruff comment during the meal. He told Sophie not to talk with her mouth full, and he narrowed his gaze at Nico when the boy walked in front of the television without saying, "Excuse me."

But he didn't only correct etiquette and issue pronouncements. He actually asked a few questions— questions that sought answers, not ones that demanded defenses like the ones he generally aimed Deke's way.

And even when he made a slighting reference to Erin's having gone "gadding off to France" as a young woman, instead of bristling defensively, Erin just laughed and agreed.

"Call it gadding if you want, but it was wonderful," she said, eyes shining. "It opened my eyes to the world outside of Elmer."

And in the face of her obvious enthusiasm, John only said gruffly, "S'pose you'd need that, coming from such a little bitty place."

As opposed, Deke thought wryly, to a metropolis as huge as Livingston.

But Erin just said, "Oh, yes. And it was the best thing that ever happened to me anyway because I met my husband there."

"Oh, yes?" John said, and Deke held his breath, wondering what comment his father might make about such a romantic pronouncement as that. But surprisingly he smiled a little wistfully. "Those are the days, aren't they?" he said. "When you've got all those hopes, all those dreams…"

Deke stared. Hopes? Dreams?

"Pass the potatoes," his father said.

* * *

As the days wore on, Erin tried simply to enjoy each day. But while it was easy to counsel herself to live in the moment, it was harder and harder not to have hopes.

Especially when she was falling deeper and deeper in love.

She had always loved the young man Deke had been. She'd admired him, dreamed about him, respected him. And as unrequited as her love had been, she had never really regretted it because, as she had once told Nathalie, loving Deke had taught her what to value, what to look for in the man she married.

She had found those qualities in Jean-Yves. And for twelve years she had loved him with all her heart. Even after his death she had persisted in her love. She still loved him even now, but not in the same way.

Now those feelings focused once again on Deke because all the things about him that she'd once loved were still there. They had developed and matured even as Deke had.

He was the man now she had once thought he could become—a strong, committed, loving father, a still-devoted son trying to please his stubborn old man, a talented photographer, a gentleman, a generous lover, a wonderful friend.

Everything she wanted.

And as the days went on, as he stayed, as he became a part of their lives, she dared to hope. She let down her defenses a little more every day.

She gave her heart to Zack. How could she not? Deke's little son was so openly adoring, so eager to be with her, so ready to call her Mama.

She winced every time he did it around Deke,

expecting him to tell Zack that Mama wasn't her name. But he didn't. He acted like he didn't notice.

Maybe he didn't. Erin didn't know. She didn't know how Deke felt at all. Well, no, that wasn't quite true. She knew he liked her. He talked with her the way he always had. He joked with her, teased her, confided in her about his father, about his son.

She was still his "best friend."

Even more, she knew he would still be happy to go to bed with her. She'd seen the way he looked at her when he thought she wasn't noticing. There was a hunger in his eyes that, if she only gave the word, she was sure he would be happy to assuage.

Truth to tell, there was a hunger inside Erin, too, that seemed to grow more insistent every day. When she was with him, she wanted to touch him. The other night she had given in to temptation and kissed his cheek. But she wanted to do a lot more than that.

She wanted to put her fingers on his arm, to slip her hand inside his shirt, to unbuckle his belt and—

Heavens, she could make herself crazy just thinking about it!

Don't! she told herself. *Stop!*

But somewhere along the line *don't* and *stop* faded away and became *Don't stop!* And as she lay awake every night, tossing and turning, she couldn't stop remembering the love they'd shared.

She wanted it again. She wanted it forever.

She had turned him away from her bed when he'd come back. She'd told him she didn't want that. What if now she told him she did?

Another sleepless night. Two. Tossing. Turning. Wishing.

Hoping.

They had so much in common—their interests, their work, their children, their mutual compatibility in bed. Everything they'd had years ago—and more. Deke looked at her with desire now. He had learned the secrets of her body just as she had learned his.

But did he want her forever?

Did he love her the way she loved him?

Chapter 11

"Is it time yet?"

"Can we go yet?"

"Can't we start yet?"

The Elmer Christmas Pageant was *the* community event of the year. From the time Erin had been old enough to toddle until she'd gone away to Paris, she'd been a part of it. And now her children were.

They'd been buzzing with excitement all month. And ever since they'd got up this morning, they'd been fidgeting, unable to sit still, anxiously awaiting the program that night.

"What if I forget my lines?" Gabriel demanded. He was going to recite "The Night before Christmas" as it was pantomimed by the seventh and eighth grades.

"You won't," Erin assured him. He'd said it so many

times around the house that she was sure *she* could prompt him if he had a memory lapse.

"What if I trip on my wings?" Sophie fretted. She was an angel in the Christmas story, and a townsperson in the Frosty the Snowman sequence.

"Keep your wings close to your body," Erin advised. She'd learned that during her own tenure as one of the heavenly host, thirty-odd years ago. "And shuffle your feet."

"What if I throw up?" Nicolas said. He looked a little green around the gills, though whether from prepageant nerves or too many Christmas cookies, Erin wasn't sure. He was a shepherd at the manger in one sequence, which shouldn't be worrying him. But he was Parson Brown in the "Winter Wonderland" piece, which meant he had to wear a frock coat and look like he was performing a marriage.

"Celie showed you what to do," his mother reassured him. "You'll be fine."

"I might not be," Nicolas said. "Uncle Taggart says *anything* can happen at the Elmer Christmas pageant!"

"And probably already has," Erin said.

The Elmer Christmas pageant was probably as old as the town of Elmer itself. The pageant, which was usually put on the last Sunday night before Christmas, was religious and secular, traditional and innovative and, Erin was sure, absolutely politically incorrect.

Fortunately, since it was neither government funded nor compulsory, no one cared.

It did what it was intended to do—bring the community together—and it was one of the things Erin had most looked forward to when she and the children had moved back to Montana.

You never knew what was going to happen at the Elmer Christmas pageant. When Erin was a little girl, two shepherds had got into a fist fight and the manger had fallen on top of them. The year before she'd gone to Paris, Tom Dixon and Margie Kelly had announced their engagement after getting "mock married" by Parson Brown.

A couple of years ago, Taggart had told her, he'd been shanghaied into playing Joseph and the very pregnant Mary McLean—now Mary Holt—had gone into labor right on stage! Gus had spirited her off to the hospital, had stood by her during the birth and had married her two months later.

Last year Erin's old journalist friend Charlie Seeks Elk had been coerced by mayor Polly McMaster into directing the pageant. People were still talking about what a fantastic job Charlie had done creating photo shim backdrops for all the production pieces.

This year the directing job had gone to Polly's sister, Celie Tucker. And for weeks everyone had wondered how she could possibly top Charlie's fantastic sets. And the answer was, of course, she couldn't.

But Celie had her own strengths—which became apparent when the house lights went down and the stage lights came up and, as Jace Tucker began to narrate, everyone got a good look at the man in the bathrobe leading the donkey.

"Ohmigod, it's Sloan!"

"Look! It's Gallagher!"

"Sloan Gallagher's playin' Joseph!" The words were whispered over and over around the hall as the amazed and delighted citizens of Elmer saw that their very own Hollywood heart throb had come home for Christmas.

"An', good grief, that's Polly playin' Mary!"

Sure enough, Sloan's wife, former mayor and postmistress of Elmer, was seated, red-faced with embarrassment, but definitely smiling, on the back of the donkey Sloan led. Everyone was enchanted—and thrilled—that Polly and Sloan hadn't forgotten their "roots," that they'd come back to be part of Elmer's celebration.

And, Erin realized, looking at Polly, to let Elmer become part of theirs. Because the smile she saw on Polly's face when she looked at Sloan was a smile of such love and happiness that she knew their marriage was, indeed, cause for celebration.

Erin felt a pang of envy just looking at them. Two years younger than Polly, Erin had known her and her first husband, Lew, all her life. She'd gone to Polly and Lew's wedding. She remembered the birth of their daughter Sara. In her romantic daydreams, Erin had thought that maybe she and Deke could follow Polly and Lew's example.

Of course they hadn't. But she'd thought of Polly and Lew often over the years. And the news of Lew's death in a plane crash some years ago had touched her deeply.

Later, when her own Jean-Yves had been killed, Erin had felt a deep bond with Polly McMaster. A widow left with plenty of young kids, Polly would have known exactly how Erin was feeling. Aching. Bereft. Alone.

And now…now Polly had found a new love. She had moved on. She was alone no longer. And watching her with Sloan, smiling at him, being smiled at in return, Erin ached to do the same.

Last year at this time who would ever have thought

that Sloan Gallagher and Polly McMaster would be together?

No one. Not a soul.

For that matter, who would have thought Jace Tucker and Celie O'Meara would now be man and wife?

Nobody. It was inconceivable. Less likely even than she and Deke!

And how unexpected and unlikely were they?

Erin slanted a glance at the man sitting next to her, the man balancing his unplanned, unexpected, unlikely son on his knee, the man whose arm stretched along the back of her chair and now and again brushed against her shoulders. The man she had walked away from years ago because it seemed that in this lifetime he would never love her.

But entirely unexpected possibilities could become realities.

If a child could become a savior, if the most unlikely people could fall in love, then who knew what miracles could happen?

Erin dared to hope. After all, wasn't that what Christmas was all about?

The phone rang just as Deke was getting ready to close the store on Christmas Eve afternoon. It was the one day of the year the store closed early.

"Five o'clock," his father had said when he'd talked to him the day he'd come home from the hospital. "You can close at five. And not a minute before."

It was three minutes to five now. No one had been in for a last-minute onion or bottle of rubbed sage or can of chicken broth in half an hour. He'd sent Evelyn home with the last three packages of cranberries and

Leo with a goose to take to his daughter's tomorrow. He'd just swept the floor and wiped out the meat display case and put everything into the refrigerated locker. He'd closed out the register and noted the totals and was just reaching for his jacket when the phone rang.

He made a bet with himself on his way to answer it. Nettie Wilbur, he guessed. She had been in three times today for things she'd forgotten. Or maybe Earlene Love, who had ordered a turkey and had gone to Red Lodge to her sister's instead, was calling to tell him he could sell her bird. Or—happy thought—it was Erin telling him to hurry home, that she could hardly wait until he got there, that she loved him, that—

It rang again.

Deke picked it up. "Malone's."

"Thought you might've left," his father said.

Deke's teeth came together with a snap. "We close at five," he said through them. "I was busy."

"Wanted you to stop by on your way home."

"Why? Does Mom need something?"

"Your mother is at the old folks' home visitin' Mrs. Pace." Their former next-door neighbor, he meant. Mrs. Pace didn't have family in town anymore, so Deke's mother made it a point to visit her on holidays.

"Then why—"

"I'll see you in a few minutes," his father said and hung up.

The adolescent, rebellious Deke, who was still alive and kicking deep down in his thirty-seven-year-old soul, ground his teeth at the peremptory summons. He took his time. If the old man thought he could run everything his way, he was wrong.

But, in the end, of course, Deke went. He had

intended to stop by, anyway. He had a stack of presents to deliver from himself and Zack and Erin and her kids.

And maybe, he told himself as he drove over to his parents' house, that was all his dad wanted—to have him stop to pick up gifts for them.

Yeah, right. More likely the old man had heard a few complaints about the store since he'd been out of the hospital and wanted to make sure Deke heard them, too. Just one more way to enhance his holiday.

His father's bed was still in the family room. But he was dressed and sitting in his recliner when Deke arrived with a stack of presents in his arms. It was half past five—the clock was just chiming as he came in the room. John glanced at it, then at his son. Deke half expected the old man to complain that he'd dallied too long on his way over. But he didn't. He just nodded.

"Merry Christmas, ho ho ho," Deke said, setting the presents on the table, then turning around and pasting a determined smile on his face.

"Merry Christmas yourself," his father said. He wasn't smiling, but he wasn't scowling, either. He nodded his head toward some gifts beside their small tree. "Those are for you to take. Your mother wrapped them."

"Right. Thanks." Deke started toward them.

"That's not why I asked you to come," his father said.

Deke stopped. He looked at his old man.

A muscle was ticking in his father's temple. His knuckles were white as he gripped the arms of the chair. Deke tried not to think about what was coming next. Didn't want to know how he'd failed this time. Couldn't even guess.

"Want to go up to the attic," his father said.

"What?" Deke stared.

The old man was shoving himself to his feet, the knuckles whiter than ever with the strain. "You deaf?" he snapped. "Said I wanted to go to the attic."

"You can't go to the attic," Deke said as his father shuffled toward the hall. "You can't climb stairs!"

"Well, flyin's out. You got any better ideas?"

"Dad!" Deke went after him, but stopped just short of touching him. There was no way he would physically restrain his father from doing anything. "Dad, the doc said you're not supposed to exert. He said you have to take care of yourself."

John turned on the bottom step, so that he and Deke were eye to eye. "That's just exactly what I'm doin'. Now are you comin', or are you just goin' to stand there flappin' your jaw?"

"Fine," Deke muttered. "Lead on."

Slowly, excruciatingly, his father began to mount the stairs. It took an effort for him to make the second floor. He stopped and held on to the newel post when he got there. His skin looked gray.

"Tell me what you want," Deke insisted. "I'll get it for you."

But his father shook his head. He didn't waste his breath on words, just opened the door that led upstairs and began to climb again.

It was cold and drafty in the attic. His father was breathing hard by the time he got there. Shivering, too.

"Wait," Deke said, bolted back down the steps, grabbed his father's fleece jacket from the closet and raced back up again. "If you're going to be a damn fool, at least be a warm one."

Something flickered in his father's face. Deke

wasn't sure what. But the old man pulled on the jacket. "Thanks." Then he looked around, got his bearings and nodded toward the far end. "Over here."

The attic was stacked with boxes, with old furniture, with racks of summer clothes and used sports gear. He spotted his old hockey skates, his sisters' prom dresses under plastic, his mother's knitting machine, stacks and stacks of empty canning jars. There was his grandmother's old curtain stretcher and the photo of his grandfather at the Denver Stock Show when he'd bought the prize beef back in 1947. There were things Deke recalled and things he never remembered seeing before.

"What are you looking for?" he asked when his father started moving boxes out of the way.

"It's here," John said. "Back here. Give me a hand."

Shaking his head, wondering how he was going to explain to his mother that his father had wanted to die in a drafty attic on Christmas Eve, Deke began to move boxes, too.

"What—?" he began to ask again.

"It's for Zack," his father said. He slumped in Great-grandpa's old rocking chair and watched as Deke moved the last boxes.

"For Zack?" They were looking for some old toy?

"There."

It wasn't a toy at all. Not really. What John was pointing at was a child-size easel. Maybe a little bigger than for a boy Zack's size, but a real easel. One Deke had certainly never seen before.

"Boy likes to draw," John said. "He should have it."

"Where'd it come from? I don't remember it." Deke stared at it, baffled, then looked around at his father.

Blue eyes just like Zack's, just like his own, looked back at him. "It was mine."

Deke simply stared. He tried to put the two to-gether—the child-size easel and the pragmatic hard-bitten man.

John leaned forward from the rocker and picked up a large flat folio that was leaning against one of the boxes. Silently he handed it to Deke.

It was dusty and musty. Deke wrinkled his nose as he unfastened the flap and opened it. In it were sketchbooks, drawings, paintings. He set the folio down and one by one began to draw them out.

The earliest sketches and paintings were childish and awkward. But there was intensity in them, passion, determination. Later ones were strong and daring and bold. Not tutored, but promising.

Deke went through them slowly, noting the raw energy, the undisciplined but clear talent at work.

His first instinct was to ask who'd done them. But he didn't need to. And if he hadn't already known, the artist's initials were at the bottom of each page. JTM.

John Thomas Malone.

He swallowed. He studied. Then slowly Deke looked up and stared at his father again, as if he'd never seen him before. "Why did…" No. More important, "Why *didn't*…?"

His father had had so much talent, such an obvious gift—one that Deke had never even dreamed existed—and he'd never pursued it.

John shrugged. "I got married, had you. Other things mattered more."

There was no rancor in his words, and if there was a hint of regret, there was no resentment.

"Responsibility," Deke said slowly.

His father nodded. Their gazes met. And for the first time, Deke began to understand the man his father had become.

He was a father himself now. And if he had to choose between his art and his son, he knew which he would choose. And he wouldn't regret it, either.

He smiled, blinked back wholly unexpected tears, and knew the gift was his as much as Zack's. "Thanks."

A faint smile touched his father's face, too, as he nodded. "Takes one to know one, isn't that what they say?" He held out a hand to his son.

Deke took it—and drew his father to his feet. They stood inches apart. It was so cold he could see their breath mingling. Then he stepped closer and hesitantly, tentatively wrapped the old man in a hug. A bare second later, he felt his own breath squeezed out of him as his father hugged him back.

Then John stepped back and cleared his throat. He didn't look at Deke, but at the pictures he had painted and the sketches he had drawn. "I was right," he said, his voice raspy, "doin' what I did. It was my responsibility." He drew a breath. "But I shouldn't have expected you to do the same. You didn't have the same responsibilities."

Deke stared. Had his father just admitted he'd been wrong?

"Dad?"

His father looked at him. A corner of his mouth lifted a fraction. "You take good pictures."

Then he reached out and took the folio from Deke's hands. Carefully, neatly he put the sketchbooks and paintings back in it. He wrapped it back up and put it on the shelf where it had been for years and years. Then he turned his back and stumped toward the stairs.

"Cold up here. Like to freeze my ears off. What're you waitin' for? Bring the easel for the boy and we'll go down."

Deke put the easel under the Christmas tree that night after the kids were all tucked in their beds.

"Where'd you get that?" Erin asked when he brought it in from the truck.

"My dad gave it to me. It's for Zack."

She looked at him quizzically, and Deke smiled. He'd been smiling all evening, still bemused, still amazed, still holding on to the astonishing events of this afternoon as his very own secret—as his greatest source of hope.

If his father could change—if John Malone could see things differently after all these years, if he could unbend, admit he'd been wrong—well then, as far as Deke was concerned, *anything* could happen.

Erin could love him.

He hoped. He prayed. And soon—tomorrow, on Christmas—he would ask.

But tonight he would be like a child again, living in anticipation. The children had been bouncing off the walls this evening—especially Nicolas, whose enthusiasm was contagious and who kept telling Zack all about Santa coming down the chimney and putting presents out for them to open in the morning.

"Santa?" Zack's eyes had grown wide and wondering. "Presents?"

And Nicolas had nodded, eyes like saucers, too. "He puts them under the tree in the dark and we'll get up really early and when we put the lights on in the tree, you'll see he's been here."

Getting Zack to sleep after that had been a trick. "See presents?" he'd said. "See Santa?"

"You can't see Santa. But you'll see that he's been here in the morning," Deke had told him. "You just have to wait."

Now as he watched Erin playing Santa, putting gifts under the tree, filling stockings, then turning and smiling at him, he was waiting, too. He thought this anticipation was even better.

She stepped back and surveyed the room. "There now." She sighed her satisfaction. "Now it looks like Christmas."

Deke nodded. "It does." And he dared to slip an arm around her and draw her under the sprig of mistletoe that Sophie had hung in the doorway.

Erin's eyes grew wide now, and he felt her tremble. He didn't want to ruin things. Didn't want to push. So he swallowed his desire and settled for giving her a gentle kiss.

"Merry Christmas."

Deke wasn't sure what woke him.

A noise? The faint glow of light from downstairs? Reindeer feet on the rooftop?

Might have been. He didn't know. The clock on the bedside table said 3:18. Automatically he looked toward Zack's mattress to see if the little boy had rolled off as he often did during the night.

Zack wasn't there.

Groaning, Deke sat up and looked around the darkened room. His son had been known to roll halfway across it in his sleep. But he didn't see any sleeping bodies anywhere. Raking his fingers through his hair, he stumbled up and padded out into the hall.

There was, in fact, a light coming from downstairs.

Erin had gone to bed at the same time he had. Had she got back up because she couldn't sleep? Because she was missing Jean-Yves? Because she had forgotten to put something under the tree? Or had Zack awakened her?

Deke headed down the hallway. As he reached the stairs, Erin came out of her room.

She started sleepily and frowned at him. "What're you—"

"What are *you*—" he countered.

Her eyes narrowed as she looked down the stairs toward the soft glow. "If Nicolas is up already—"

"I can't find Zack."

"Come on."

They crept down together.

A soft golden glow spilled from the multicolored tiny lights of the Christmas tree. And there, in the middle of the carpet, gazing up in rapt wonder at the sight knelt Zack in his blanket sleeper.

Zack had come downstairs in the middle of the night? Zack had plugged in the tree lights?

Deke looked at Erin. Erin looked at Deke. Then quietly together they went and sat down beside him. He turned to look at them each in turn. Then he smiled.

"Look," he said, pointing at the tree. "Light."

"Light," Deke agreed.

"Light," Erin echoed.

And when, half an hour later Deke carried his sleeping son back to bed, he stood for a long moment and stared out the window at the night sky—at the stars overhead and thought about light and hope and promises and miracles.

He thought about Erin. About family. About the past and the future. He thought about Thanksgiving and how he'd wondered what coming home would bring.

More than he'd ever expected. More than he'd ever hoped for.

Then, smiling with anticipation, he slept.

Of course it wasn't the best Christmas ever.

But it was close. It was warm and filled with joy and togetherness and memories and hopes. Nicolas got them up at six-thirty. Erin sent him back to bed with his stocking and told him eight was a more reasonable hour.

He lasted until seven. Then Gabe awakened and Sophie, and Zack went toddling down the hall announcing, "Santa come!"

Santa had indeed come. He'd brought Gabe and Nicolas hockey skates and Sophie a saddle. He'd brought Zack a wooden train set and some toddler-size Legos. Gabe had given him paints and Sophie had got him a roll of paper. Nico bought him big fat brushes and lots of stubby colored markers. And, of course, there was the easel.

"From Grandpa," Deke told him, clipped the paper on it, gave him the paints and let him go to it.

Who knew what he painted? Who cared? Someday, Deke guessed, it would be obvious.

But for now the intensity was there. The focus. The passion.

The Legos sat. So did the trains, while Zack painted picture after picture.

"Imagine your father thinking of that," Erin said, smiling fondly as she watched Zack attacking yet another piece of paper with single-minded vigor.

And Deke just smiled. "Will wonders never cease?"

They went to church in the morning, all six of them together. They ate dinner at home in the afternoon as if they were a family. Then they made the rounds—visiting her parents and his, then his sister's family and her brother's family. It was late and the kids were exhausted by the time they got home. Zack fell asleep in the car.

"Don't wake me up early," Nicolas mumbled when he fell into bed, his new hockey skates under his arm.

Erin laughed. "What a difference a day makes." She kissed him good-night, then went to kiss Sophie.

"C'était magnifique, n'est-ce pas?" Sophie murmured when Erin bent to kiss her good-night.

"Mmm," she agreed. "It was."

"It was good, wasn't it?" Gabriel said to her. He didn't have his skates *in* his bed, but they were on the bookshelf alongside.

"It was good," Erin agreed.

But Gabriel leaned up on one elbow. "Not just Christmas," he clarified. "Good we came."

To Elmer, he meant. To America. Erin nodded. "Yes."

She brushed a hand over his dark hair and smiled wistfully. It had been far better than she'd ever expected. And yet...she wanted more.

She peeked into Zack and Deke's room on her way past. Zack was fast asleep. Deke wasn't there. She tiptoed in and dropped a kiss on Zack's soft cheek, whispered her love to him, and then, still wanting—still hoping—she went downstairs.

Deke had built a fire. The only light in the living room came from the fireplace and the tree. The room was warm and welcoming and Deke, straightening up in front of the fire, looked warm and welcoming—and serious—too.

Erin smiled and held out her hands toward the fire. "Wonderful. It's been a wonderful day."

"It has," Deke agreed. He paused, then rocked back on his heels and forward again. "It's been a wonderful month. Season, I mean—Christmas." He sounded strained. Nervous?

Erin's heart quickened. "Yes," she said. "I've enjoyed it. It was a lot better than I thought it would be," she added, wanting to give him some encouragement.

He took it. "So," he said, "why don't we get married?"

Erin's heart leaped. It soared. It did triple axels and somersaults and a dozen high-flying loops.

"Married?" She felt breathless.

"Married," Deke said firmly. "It makes sense, doesn't it?"

"Sense?" Erin echoed faintly.

He nodded. "Absolutely. It would be good for your kids and good for mine. We can help each other out that way. It's worked out well this month, hasn't it?" He didn't stop for an answer, just went right on. "And it can be even better when I'm not at the store anymore," he told her. "When we're both shooting, we can help each other out there, as well. Compatible interests and all that? Right?"

Compatible interests? Was that what they had?

"I'd move back up here, of course," Deke told her.

"I wouldn't expect you to come down to New Mexico. I know you came back from Paris because you want to be here near your folks. And—" he shrugged "—I think it might be a good thing if I was closer, too, now that my folks are getting older." He ran out of breath, apparently, because he stopped then and looked at her expectantly. Hopefully.

And Erin just stood there, stunned. Because even though they were all very good reasons, very logical, sensible reasons—none of them was the right reason. He never said he loved her.

Because, of course, Erin realized at that moment, he didn't love her.

Had never loved her. Except, as always, as his "good friend"—his "buddy."

But she loved him. Desperately. Terribly. And the knowledge that he still didn't reciprocate crushed her. And all she could think to do was say, "That's all?"

"All?" Deke stared at her, equally stunned. Then he fidgeted, looking uncomfortable. He hesitated, fumbled, shrugged, raked a hand through his hair.

"I can't be—" he began, then stopped and shook his head.

And the words she wanted never came.

"Fine," he said, voice taut, body stiff now. "Never mind. Sorry I asked. I didn't mean to offend you." A muscle was ticking in his jaw.

"You didn't—" She started to protest, but tears pricked her eyes and her voice broke and she couldn't lie and say he hadn't.

Deke jammed his hands in his pockets. "There's no point in staying then. Merry Christmas. We'll leave in the morning."

* * *

In the morning they did just that.

He had the truck packed and Zack dressed by the time the kids came downstairs.

"You're what? You're leaving?" Sophie was distraught. "You can't!" She started to cry.

"You can't go," Nico said. "We need you here!"

"I thought you were going to teach me how to shoot," Gabe said, looking mutinous.

Deke took it all stoically and Erin didn't help in the slightest. She couldn't. Simply couldn't say a word. He was leaving. And taking Zack!

"I have to go," was all Deke said. He shook hands with Gabriel. He kissed Sophie. He gave Nicolas a hug.

"Bye?" Zack said, waving and looking bewildered as Deke carried him out of the house.

Gabe gave Erin a mutinous look as if to ask, What did you do to drive him away?

And Erin wiped her palms on her jeans and said, "We always knew Deke had a life back in New Mexico and that he wasn't going to stay here forever."

She prayed Deke wouldn't contradict her—and traitorously her heart almost wished he would.

Of course he didn't. He bundled Zack into his car seat and gave her one long last unreadable look. Then he got into his truck and headed out.

Erin got through the day without breaking. She was brisk and efficient and she managed to be cheery and capable and competent, getting through the day minute by minute with the same resilience that she had after Jean-Yves had died.

As with Jean-Yves, she only cracked after she went to bed that night.

She tossed and turned. She couldn't sleep. She paced the floor. Had she been wrong to say no? Should she have taken the half loaf of his regard and their "compatible interests" instead of holding out for love?

Oh, God, this was terrible! It hurt. *She* hurt! She ended up in the room where Deke had slept. She sat on the bed. She hugged the pillow to her.

It smelled of Deke.

Tears started to fall.

It had been this way with Jean-Yves. She had got through that. She would get through this.

But somehow this was harder. You couldn't change death. But Deke wasn't dead. And she would go through her life without him—knowing she could have had him, and that he was alive and well and in New Mexico.

Zack had learned a lot of words in the past month. He said them over and over on the way south.

"Gabe," he said. "So-fee! Nico! Where's Nico? Sammy? Gran'pa! Want Gran'pa!" But mostly he said, "Go home. Want Mama! Where Mama?"

Mama.

Of course he meant Erin.

Past Billings, past Hardin, past Sheridan and Kaycee, he babbled on about Gabe and Nico and Sofee and Mama.

Always Mama. Mama. Mama.

Erin. Erin. Erin.

Zack didn't remember Violet. If she'd ever been Mama to him, it wasn't Violet he called for now. He wanted the woman that Gabe and Sophie and Nicolas called Mama. The woman he called Mama. The woman he loved like a mother.

The woman Deke loved, period.

The woman who didn't love him.

If she'd loved him at all she'd have said yes, wouldn't she?

If she'd thought there was even a possibility that she might have eventually been able to feel for him what she'd felt for Jean-Yves, surely she would have given them that chance.

But she hadn't.

She'd just listened to his reasons, had stood there in the living room staring at him as if he were some sort of lunatic while he'd tried to think of all the reasons he could to convince her to marry him, to give them a chance. And then she'd said, "That's all?"

All? Hell no, it wasn't all.

He loved her.

He hadn't said that, though. Hadn't dared. Had been afraid to admit it.

And yet now, every mile farther south he drove, he felt more clearly the ache that turning away from that love brought. He couldn't get away from it. He was carrying it with him.

He should have said it then. He couldn't.

He shifted uncomfortably against the seat. His gaze met their mirrored image in the rearview mirror and he remembered the last time his eyes had locked onto a pair just like them—his father's eyes. And he was struck once more how very like his father he was.

Not just in looks, either.

On Christmas Eve John had given him the easel. He'd said at last, "You take good pictures."

He hadn't been able to say, "I love you." He'd expected Deke to understand. And for the first time Deke had. But he had longed to hear the words just the same.

Had Erin longed to hear the words from him?

Was that what she'd meant when she'd asked, "That's all?"

Stunned, Deke hit the brakes. Oh, God.

It was, Erin thought, as she dragged herself downstairs the next morning feeling like she'd been run over by a truck, déjà vu all over again.

The hollow, aching feeling she'd felt after Jean-Yves's death was back. It would get better, she reminded herself as she started breakfast. Got down the oatmeal. Got out the pot. Turned on the water.

Time healed. But time didn't hurry.

And until it did, she would hurt.

It didn't help that the kitchen was like a funeral parlor. The boys were going skating with friends, and Sophie was spending the day in Bozeman with Felicity and Becky at her grandma's. But none of them seemed eager. They poked at their toast in silence.

"Maybe you can take that high chair back to Felicity when they pick you up," Erin said to Sophie.

Sophie just looked at her reproachfully. And Erin could read her expression perfectly clearly. *That high chair is Zack's.*

Zack's not coming back, she wanted to say. She felt she had to say it about a hundred times a day at least in her head to come to terms with it. She just wasn't sure she had the energy to say it aloud this morning and then deal with Sophie's pain.

But before she could decide whether she did or not, there were sudden quick steps on the porch and the back door opened.

They all stared. Then the kids whooped joyously.

"Deke!"

"Yea, Deke!"

"An' Zack! You're back!"

For he was. *They* were—man and boy—big as life and twice as beautiful, right there in her kitchen. Deke smiled at them all. He ruffled Gabriel's and Nicolas's hair and gave Sophie a squeeze. But his eyes went straight to Erin.

"Forget something?" she asked, holding on to her composure with every ounce of determination she had.

He was stubble-jawed and bloodshot-eyed and he looked as if he'd been driving for twenty-four hours straight. But his eyes never wavered as he nodded. "I did," he told her. He handed Zack to Gabe and crossed the room to face her squarely. "I forgot to tell you that I love you."

Erin dropped the spoon in the oatmeal pot. She stared, astonished and transfixed, disbelieving at the same time her heart was leaping for joy. In all the scenarios she'd conjured in the month they'd been together, she'd never conjured this one.

"You do?" she said. She felt faint.

"I do." It was as much a marriage vow as any he would ever make. He gave her the words at last—and the truth. "That's the only important reason for asking you to marry me."

Erin had always prized her composure, but she lost it then. Tears rolled down her cheeks.

The kids gaped.

"Mama?" Sophie said worriedly.

"Es tu bien?" Nicolas demanded.

"Are you okay?" Gabe asked.

And Erin, smiling through her tears as she let the oatmeal burn, put her arms around the man she loved and told her children, "I've never been better in my life."

"Me, neither," Deke whispered against her hair. He held her tight, kissed her desperately, then opened his arms to the rest of them and drew them into a family hug.

"Mama," Zack said, patting her, and she looked up to find him beaming at her. One by one he touched them all. "Mama. Gabe. So-fee. Nico. Dad."

And then he stretched out his arms and smiled, satisfied. "We're home."

Epilogue

They were alone.

"Hard to imagine," Erin said, looking around the empty kitchen.

"Hard to believe," Deke agreed gruffly. They'd been married a month and he'd barely had a chance to be alone with his wife. He was still running the grocery store though his dad was back two mornings a week. But this morning Deke was letting Leo and Evelyn handle the store, so he didn't have to go in until noon. A half hour ago the big kids had gone off to school, and his mother had just driven off with Zack in tow, intending to take him to their place. Deke was going to pick him up this afternoon.

"So he and Grandpa can color together," Carol had said when she'd called to request Zack's visit.

Something else that was hard to believe—that his

father wanted to bond with his son. Deke was glad. Coming home had been the right thing to do.

And not just for Zack and the old man.

"So," Erin said briskly, "what shall we tackle first? The wallpaper? Painting Zack's room?"

"I was thinking about our room," Deke said.

She frowned as she put the dishes in the dishwasher. "Our room? I know you aren't crazy about the wallpaper in our room. It is a little girly looking with all those tiny flowers. But there is a stripe, Deke."

"I can live with the wallpaper," he assured her. "I have a different project in mind."

Erin grimaced. "You don't want to refinish the floor do you? Bare floors are pretty but they're so much colder than carpets."

"I don't want to refinish the floor," Deke said. He took her hand. "Come on. I'll show you."

"What?" she said as he drew her with him up the stairs and into the bedroom.

The wallpaper was too girly as far as he was concerned. Tiny sprigs of violets were not really his style—even if they came with the occasional purple stripe. But he could live with violets. He could live with ruffles here and there. There were ruffles on the pillow shams. Hell, he could even live with pillow shams. And lace curtains.

As long as he could live with Erin.

"What?" she said again as he steered her into the bedroom and turned her to face him.

"This," he said, and touched his lips to hers. "I have been waiting and waiting and waiting for this." He punctuated each *waiting* with a kiss. He tugged her shirttails out of her jeans and slid his fingers beneath, reveling in the warm silky smoothness of her skin.

"Oh!" she said.

"Ah," she said.

"Mmm," she said. And she was kissing him back then, doing a very thorough job of removing his shirt. She was so much better at buttons than he was.

"Wait," he muttered. "Slow down." But when she did, he found he didn't want to. He wanted her—now. And when he said, "Never mind slowing down," she laughed and unfastened his jeans and yanked them down.

They tumbled onto the bed, shedding clothes, stroking skin, stoking flames of need and desire. They made love quickly and urgently. Then, because they really did have time, for once, they made love again. And this time they took it slow, enjoying a leisurely thoroughness that left them both limp and temporarily sated.

And afterward they lay wrapped in each other's arms, Erin's head on Deke's shoulder, her legs tangling with his, her hand playing with a line of hair on his chest. "Well, now," she murmured. "That was nice."

Deke raised a brow. "Nice?"

"Mmm. Well, you know…" She yawned, then tipped her head to grin up at him.

He nuzzled his nose in her soft hair. "I know." He sighed, then smiled. "It sure beats going in to the store this morning."

"Your father would be shocked to hear you say that."

"Maybe not. The old man is all for duty. But to him duty to wife and family was always paramount. He might even give me the John Malone seal of approval."

"Don't get carried away," Erin cautioned. "Just

because you're in his good books for a change." She rolled over and looked up at him. "He is very pleased you're moving back here."

"Told you that, did he?"

He certainly hadn't said so to Deke. Not that Deke had been expecting him to. He and his father were at peace at the moment, but they weren't sharing their deepest secrets and probably never would. Their one encounter in the attic on Christmas Eve was probably as close and as deep as they would ever get.

"It's obvious," Erin told him. "He's making plans for things to do with Zack and C.J. He's going to take them fishing. He's going to play catch with them. Paint with them."

"Sort brussels sprouts with them."

"Maybe. It could be worse. You survived."

"After a fashion."

"He's very proud of you."

"Right."

"He bought your arroyo photos."

Deke stared at her. "He did what?"

His four-part series of photos of an arroyo during a flash flood last year were quite different from his usual focus on space and horizon. The narrow confines of the arroyo in the first shot had been quiet, spare, peaceful, empty. The second shot showed a sudden summer storm building, lightning crackling, rain pounding. The third was of the arroyo filled with a deluge of rushing churning water that tumbled branches, rolled rocks, wreaked havoc, sweeping aside everything in its path. The fourth shot, taken only hours later, showed the arroyo quiet again, but different—spotted now with pools of water reflecting the beauty of the clouds in the sky, a coyote lapping at it and a tiny desert flower lifting its head, the water from the storm bringing it to life.

"Said they reminded him of you," Erin told him. She leaned toward him and kissed his jaw. "He's right."

Deke tried to digest that. It took some doing. He had a hard time imagining his father thinking symbolically—until he remembered the portfolio in the attic. He needed to keep remembering that portfolio. He needed to stop putting limits on his father, just as his father had had to stop putting limits on him.

He thought he might be able to do that, given time and the opportunity—and Erin.

Thank God he had Erin.

She'd awakened in him the man he knew he could be—the son, the father, the lover, the husband. She'd taken the raw material that was Deke Malone—with all his flaws and all his dreams and all his pain and all his hope—and with her love, she had made him whole.

He had been too young and stupid and immature and shallow to appreciate her the first time he'd had her in his life. He'd never fully valued her then. He wasn't making that mistake again.

He rolled her over and pinned her to the bed. He framed her beautiful loving face with his hands and looked deep into her eyes. "I love you," he told her in a voice hoarse with sudden emotion. "You are the best thing that ever happened to me."

She looked surprised, as if she didn't expect that kind of declaration from him. Then she smiled, too. Her gaze softened. She opened herself to him and drew him in. She gave him strength. She gave him courage. She gave him power. She gave him love.

And after he kissed her, nuzzled her and told her with utter confidence, "Together we can do anything."

Erin chuckled. "You think so?"

"I know so."

"Well, I hope you're right, because we're going to have our hands full."

Deke lifted his head and looked down at her. She was grinning at him. "Why?" he said warily.

Erin stretched and smiled. "Because in October, my darling, yours and mine are going to be joined by ours."

He gaped at her, stunned, amazed. Delighted.

"And," she went on cheerfully, "I promised Celie you'd direct the Christmas pageant this year."

* * * * *

ALWAYS POWERFUL, PASSIONATE AND PROVOCATIVE

Harlequin® Desire delivers
strong heroes, spirited heroines
and compelling love stories.

Harlequin Desire features
your favorite authors, including

ANN MAJOR, DIANA PALMER, MAUREEN CHILD AND BRENDA JACKSON.

Passionate, powerful and provocative
romances *guaranteed!*

For superlative authors, sensual stories
and sexy heroes, choose Harlequin Desire.

Harlequin *Presents*®

Seduction and Passion Guaranteed!

**The world's bestselling romance series…
The series that brings you
your favorite authors, month after month:**

Helen Bianchin
Emma Darcy
Lynne Graham
Penny Jordan
Miranda Lee
Sandra Marton
Anne Mather
Carole Mortimer
Melanie Milburne
Michelle Reid

and many more talented authors!

Wealthy, powerful, gorgeous men…
Women who have feelings just like your own…
The stories you love, set in exotic, glamorous locations…

Harlequin®

A *Romance* FOR EVERY MOOD™

Harlequin®

SPECIAL EDITION

Life, Love & Family

Emotional, compelling stories
that capture the intensity of living, loving
and creating a family in today's world.

SPECIAL EDITION FEATURES
BESTSELLING AUTHORS SUCH AS

SUSAN MALLERY
SHERRYL WOODS
CHRISTINE RIMMER
JOAN ELLIOTT PICKART

AND MANY MORE!

For a romantic, complex and emotional read,
choose Harlequin Special Edition.

Harlequin®

A *Romance* FOR EVERY MOOD™

www.ReaderService.com